THE
CONSPIRACY
OF MAGIC

STRIPES PUBLISHING LIMITED
An imprint of the Little Tiger Group
1 Coda Studios, 189 Munster Road,
London SW6 6AW

First published in Great Britain by Stripes Publishing in 2019
Text copyright © Harriet Whitehorn, 2019
Illustration © Maria Surducan, 2019

ISBN: 978-1-78895-036-7

MIX
Paper from
responsible sources
FSC® C020471

The Forest Stewardship Council® (FSC®) is a global, not-for-profit organization dedicated to
the promotion of responsible forest management worldwide. FSC defines standards based on
agreed principles for responsible forest stewardship that are supported by environmental, social,
and economic stakeholders. To learn more, visit www.fsc.org

10 9 8 7 6 5 4 3 2 1

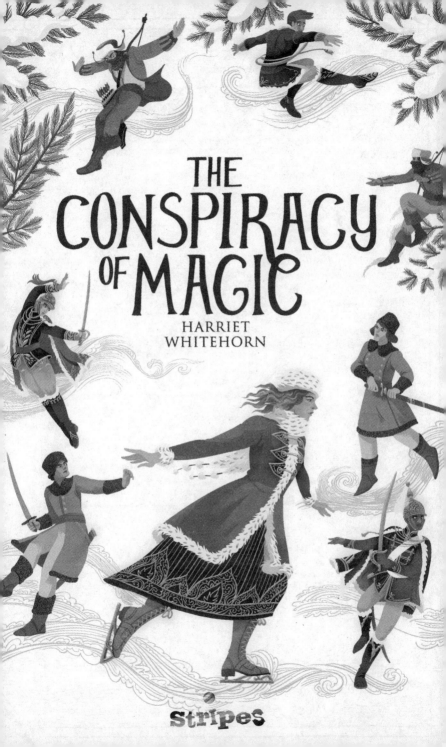

THE
CONSPIRACY
OF MAGIC

HARRIET
WHITEHORN

Stripes

TO
PINOA

Oskbar

Forest
of Thunt

Maer's
Castle

Danske

King Hoff

B U N D E R L A

Charma

Baden

Inn
of the Juggling
Hare

Aravura

Ri

THE
LONGEST WORLD

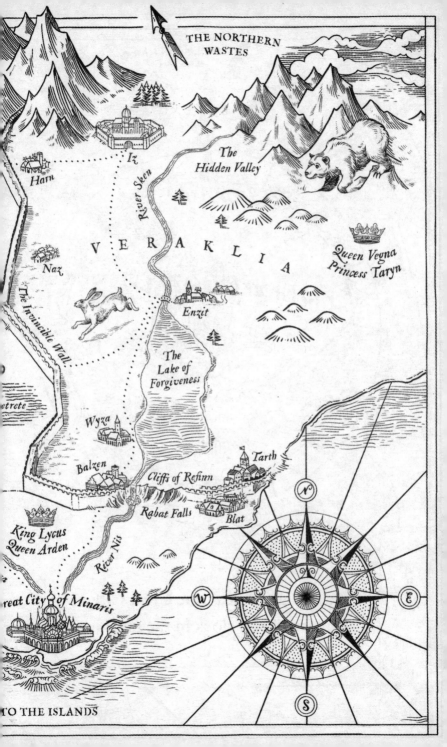

THE NORTHERN WASTES

Harn

Queen Arden

Mira

The Great City of Minaris

Vegna
Taryn

D

Metrete

Balzen
Cliffs of Return
Rabat Falls

King
Queen

Great City

N

The Square of Seas, the Great City of Minaris, Ten o'clock in the morning

I

Free Magic

The dragon circled around the Square of Seas, its blue-green scales glittering in the brittle autumn sunlight. It soared up into the air and then swooped down, narrowly missing a stone fountain. Purple smoke gushed out of its nostrils, arranging itself into the words FREE MAGIC, which hung like a banner in the still air. It was ten o'clock in the morning, a time of day when the residents of the magical district of the Great City of Minaris would normally be fast asleep after a hard night's work. But not today. Every window and doorway was crammed with gawping, gasping faces, spellbound by the dragon's antics.

What in the Longest World is going on? Cass thought as she skated into the square and saw everyone gathered around, *ooh*-ing and *aah*-ing. She had just sailed into the city's port that morning from the Mid Isles, where she had been helping to catch the last of the pirates who had been terrorizing the Islands for the previous few years. It had been a terrible voyage. It was only late autumn but the weather seemed to think that it was the middle of winter and they had hit ice storm after ice storm. Cass was exhausted and she wanted nothing more than to say hello to everyone at home, crawl into bed and sleep for a week.

She looked up at the sky and tried to see what everyone was gaping at, but it was no good – she could see nothing but blue sky. For Cass was a creature almost as rare in the Longest World as a dragon; she was an obtuse, a person immune to magic. Most people would say that it was both a blessing and a curse, but for Cass, growing up as she had at the very centre of the magical district, it had only been a source of shame.

"Goatsmilk!" a familiar voice shrieked, and a

young boy shot out from the doorstep of Cass's home, the Mansion of Fortune, and hurled himself at her.

"Lion!" Cass cried with delight as he wrapped his arms round her waist tightly. She had rescued him from the pirates the previous year and brought him back to live in Minaris with her guardian Mrs Potts.

"You look awful," he announced, taking in her pale drawn face and the dark shadows underneath her grey eyes. Even her hair, usually an explosion of blond curls, was lank and dirty-brown.

"Thanks, I know. I've spent most of the last month thinking I might die of seasickness. You on the other hand look like you've been feasting on cream and cake," she said, tickling him.

Lion let out a spluttery laugh. "Stop, stop!" he cried.

"Only if you tell me what everyone's looking at," Cass said, stopping and staring up at the sky.

"Of course; you can't see the dragon, can you?" Lion said with a slight smirk.

"You know I can't," Cass replied. "Now, tell me what's going on or I'll tickle you to death." And she held up her hands in a mock threat.

"No! No!" he squealed. "It's a magical arrest. One of the Free Magickers has been caught selling curses and he's just showing off his conjuring skills."

Cass rolled her eyes. The Free Magickers were a lawless bunch of rebel magicians who were in constant battle with the Magical Enforcers and their rules and regulations.

"Look, there's Lin with Master Brackuz," Lion continued. "They'll stop the conjuror."

Cass looked over to where Lion was pointing. She saw the familiar neat features and short blond hair of her friend Lin. She was standing a little distance away with a portly middle-aged man dressed in the amber robes of the Magical Enforcers. Lin was one of the people she'd been most looking forward to seeing. "I'm going to go and say hello."

"Do you think you should bother her?" Lion asked doubtfully.

"Oh, it'll be fine," Cass said breezily. Having spent the last few months fighting pirates, a rogue conjuror didn't seem a very great threat. "Come with me," she said, taking his hand.

"OK," Lion agreed, and they skated over to Lin and Master Brackuz. Unlike everyone else, they were ignoring the dragon and looking instead at a young man who was standing on the roof of one of the houses, moving his hands like the conductor of an orchestra.

"Cass!" Lin cried, her face lighting up when she saw her. She kissed Cass's cheek and squeezed her arm affectionately. "Master Brackuz, this is my dear friend Cassandra and her friend Lion."

Master Brackuz bowed briefly to them but his mind was elsewhere. "We should bring him in, Lin – he's had his moment of glory."

Lin nodded. "You'd better go back to the house in case he's difficult," she said to Cass.

"I don't think there's much he can do to an obtuse," Cass replied. She wanted to see her friend arrest him.

"I suppose not," Lin said. She looked at Lion.

"Oh, please can I stay?" he asked. "I can see so much better here and you know I want to be a Magical Enforcer when I'm older," he wheedled.

"I'll look after him," Cass assured them.

Lin looked doubtful but Master Brackuz cleared his throat, distracting her. "Bring him down now, Lin," he said.

"OK, stand over there," she instructed, gesturing to a spot a little way away. Lin turned her attention to the dragon and with just a twitch of a raised finger vanished it, or so Cass gathered from the collective moan of disappointment from the crowds.

"This you will be able to see, Cass," Lin said. Gazing intently at the conjuror, she muttered a few words and moved her fingers, working the spell. With his arms pinned to his sides, he began to float down through the air towards them. He was chanting, "Free Magic! Free Magic!" all the way down.

"That's very skilled, Lin," Cass said admiringly.

"You're so clever," Lion agreed.

"Perhaps you can persuade Lin to join the Magical Enforcers," Master Brackuz said to Cass. "Her talents are wasted doing fortune telling and trancing."

Lin smiled but made no reply.

The rogue conjuror landed on the ground in

front of them. He was a young man with a shock of dark hair and angry black eyes. He barely seemed to notice Cass and Lion, focusing instead on Lin and Master Brackuz.

"Petty bureaucrats!" he spat at them with furious disgust. "You are ruining the world, depriving it of the wonder and beauty of magic!"

"We are actually protecting the world from vain, selfish magicians like you who use magic maliciously for their own ends," Master Brackuz said. "Anyway, you're not a magician, you're merely a conjuror."

The conjuror narrowed his eyes in fury at him and said, "Careful who you call a conjuror, old man!" and he muttered an incantation that freed his hands in a second. He spun round to Lion and Cass, and made a gesture at Lion. In a second he had pulled the boy to him, as if he were a fish on a line. Cass was the first to react, lunging after Lion. But she froze as the magician pulled a knife out of his pocket and held it to Lion's throat. Lion stood as compliant as a doll, his eyes glazed with enchantment.

"Do not come any closer!" the magician

shouted, his voice hoarse with panicky aggression. Everyone around the square gasped and then fell silent, terrified of what would happen next.

I'm SO stupid – this is all my fault! Cass cursed herself with silent fury. *What was I thinking not sending Lion back to the house?*

She glanced over to the mansion and saw Mrs Potts and her friend Tig, their eyes wide with horror. *I'm so stupid*, she repeated to herself but she turned her focus to the magician. He was sweating, and looked like a cornered tiger. A dangerous combination, Cass knew from experience, and she stood as still as she could, anxious not to do anything that could alarm him.

"Release the boy," Lin said calmly, although Cass could hear the tremor in her voice. "He has nothing to do with this."

"Not without you letting me go," the magician shouted, his eyes wild. "Otherwise I will kill him!"

Lin and Master Brackuz exchanged glances.

"Very well, give me the boy and you may go," Master Brackuz replied calmly.

The magician glanced from one to the other of them, licking his lips nervously. "Nobody move!"

he roared at everyone, and a hundred pairs of eyes watched him drag Lion in the direction of Truelove's Way, which led out of the square to the south. When he reached the entrance of the street, the magician paused and looked around hesitantly.

He's not quite sure what to do, Cass thought, hardly daring to take a breath. *No one do anything to panic him*, she prayed. And then she watched as he glanced around again and muttered another spell. A whirlwind of thick mustard-coloured smoke appeared out of nowhere, filling the square in a moment and blinding everyone. Everyone except Cass, who saw the magician shove Lion away from him as if he were a rag doll, turn and skate off at speed. She raced over to Lion, who looked totally bewildered.

"What just happened?" he asked her. The enchantment was over, and to Cass's immense relief he appeared entirely unharmed.

"I'll tell you later," Cass said, speeding off towards Truelove's Way. "Go back to the house when the smoke clears," she shouted over her shoulder to him.

Cass could see the magician ahead of her, flying

along the narrow alley. *I have to catch him,* Cass thought, the image of him holding a knife to Lion's throat filling her with fury as she careered after him. He came to the end of the alley and shot out into the Square of Disbelievers ahead of her.

The square marked the end of the magical district and since the rest of the city kept normal working hours it was busy with Minarians going about their everyday business. Cass darted and weaved her way through the crowds, relentlessly following the magician's black coat, but as fast as she went, she could never quite reach him.

Abruptly, he swung out of the square down the busy Street of Signs, making Cass smash into a trolley piled high with trays of godran fish and island crabs.

"Watch where ya going, ya clumsy oaf!" the fishmonger bawled at her.

"Sorry!" Cass cried as she stumbled after the magician. *He's heading for the port,* she realized as he led her out on to the chaos of the Quay of Disbelievers. Moments later she let out a groan as she lost him in the swarm of people.

Cass skated up and down for a while, desperately looking for the magician but with no luck. She was just about to give up when she saw him, calmly standing on the dock, scanning the destination board for one of the Island ferries.

She skated silently up behind him and then, in a movement so swift that the young conjuror didn't know what had happened, she pinned his arms behind his back, whipped his knife out of his pocket and held it to his ribs.

"I have you, I'm afraid," Cass said in a low tone. "Now, let's not have another scene."

The magician turned to look at her, his face shocked, his angry eyes glittering. "You're an obtuse," he spat.

"I am indeed," she replied. "So you might as well save the tricks – they won't work with me."

"They used to burn obtuses as freaks of nature," he said, curling his lip at her in a sneer.

"Not any more," Cass replied coolly. "Unfortunately for you. Now, I think you'd better come with me, don't you?"

11

Cass delivered the magician back to Lin and Master Brackuz in the Square of Seas. Both the clouds of smoke and the crowds had vanished, and to look at the peaceful square you would think nothing had happened there at all.

"I can't thank you enough, young lady," Master Brackuz said, watching a gang of his enforcers take the magician away. "He made life miserable for scores of people with his curses and tricks. People only ever think of the fun of conjuring, they forget the harm that it can do if used maliciously. For instance, that young man sent a plague of giant spiders to persecute an elderly lady every night – she nearly lost her wits."

"It makes me glad to be an obtuse," Cass replied.

Master Brackuz laughed. "I also meant what I said," he added. "Please do what you can to persuade Lin to join us." Then he looked at Lin. "You are not your family, Lin, and there's no reason why you should be held responsible for their mistakes."

"That's very kind of you, Master Brackuz. But I'm not sure all enforcers would feel the same way. Besides, I'm happy as I am," Lin replied.

"Well, think about it," he said, and after bidding them goodbye he walked briskly away.

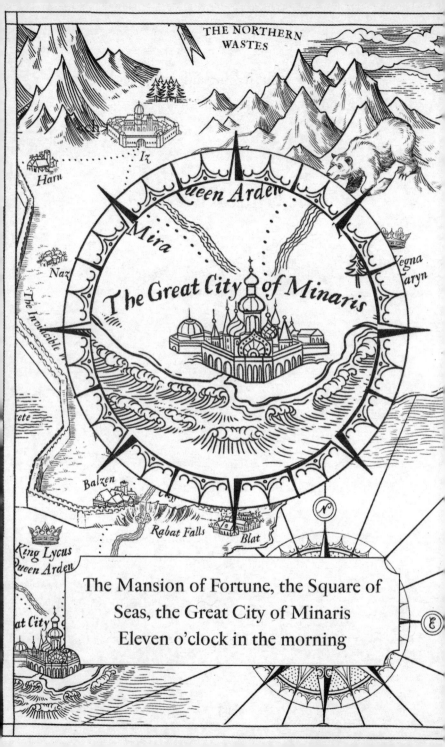

THE NORTHERN WASTES

Iz

Harn

Naz

Mira

Queen Arden

The Great City of Minaris

Vegna Caryn

The Invincible

Balzen

Rabat Falls

Blat

King Lycus Queen Arden

at City

The Mansion of Fortune, the Square of
Seas, the Great City of Minaris
Eleven o'clock in the morning

2

The Gilded Thread

Cass and Lin had grown up together so Cass knew all about Lin's family. They were once the most powerful court magicians in Minaris, only just below the royal family in wealth and importance. But after the horrors of the Magical Wars, all magicians had been stripped of their status and forbidden to practise anything but the most benign arts of fortune telling, hypnotism and trancing, which was a little like telepathy. Lin's parents and grandparents were appalled by this change in their position and had started up a revolt soon after, which with some difficulty had been squashed.

As punishment they were sent to Prison Island

for life. Only Lin and her older sister Nym, who were very young at the time, had been allowed to remain living in their mansion in the Square of Seas, under the close watch of the enforcers. Lin had missed her parents terribly but despite that she'd had a happy childhood, going to school at Mrs Papworth's Academy and playing with Cass and the other children from the square.

But Nym was different. Cass had always found Nym terrifying – she would fly off the handle at the slightest thing and bully and tease Lin cruelly. Both girls were brilliant magicians but Nym's ability seemed to come from a place of anger. So perhaps it wasn't a great surprise when, about five years before, Nym had become involved with the Free Magic movement and started tinkering with more powerful illegal magic. She was clever and got away with it for a while but as she grew more skilled, she became bolder and increasingly arrogant. Lin pleaded with her to stop but she just laughed at her. Eventually the enforcers realized what was going on, and to Lin's shame came and arrested her. But Nym managed to escape and fled Minaris.

"Do you ever hear from Nym? Do you know where she is?" Cass asked as they walked over to the Mansion of Fortune. She asked the questions tentatively as she didn't want to upset Lin by mentioning her sister.

Lin paused before replying. "Sometimes I feel her watching me," she replied. "She has grown very powerful. But no, I don't know where she is – the Farthest Lands, perhaps. It wouldn't surprise me if she was somehow involved in the Magical Uprising there."

Cass nodded. Her friend Elsba, who she had just been with in the Islands, had set sail for the Farthest Lands to go and help quell the troubles there. Elsba was part of the Company of Eight, which was a secret band of eight skilled female sword fighters whom Cass had met the year before. It was Cass's dream that one day she might become a member.

"But what about you, Cass?" Lin said. "You must be so excited to be joining Queen Arden's household! And guarding her as the queen's sword. That's so impressive."

"Thank you, but you must keep the queen's

sword bit quiet. As far as Mrs Potts, Tig and the rest of the world know, I'm a lady-in-waiting. And it's only for the queen's trip to Bunderland," Cass explained.

"Still – that's amazing. How did it come about? I know you had planned to sail on to the Far Isles. What made you change your mind?"

It was her friend Idaliz, another Company member, who had persuaded Cass over a glass of flower beer at an inn in the Mid Isles.

"Well, Idaliz is usually the queen's sword on these foreign trips," Cass explained. "But then King Lycus decided he needed her for—" Cass hesitated before saying, "He needed her for something else and then Idaliz suggested I take her place. I sailed back here with her. She's gone straight to the palace as she has to leave right away."

"And was Rip disappointed that you weren't going with him to the Far Isles? I know how close you are."

"A bit," Cass admitted but then laughed. "He's such an Islander, he couldn't believe anyone would voluntarily go anywhere cold and snowy."

When they had said goodbye, his parting words

were, "When you're stuck in a snowdrift in the shivering cold, Cass, think of me in the Far Isles. I'll be basking like a lizard in the sunshine."

He would nearly be there by now, Cass thought.

Lin's voice brought her back to the present, as she asked, "And will you sail out to meet him when you're back?"

"That's the plan. Right after the Mid-Winter Feast. It should only take about six weeks if I take a fast boat," Cass said as they arrived at her house and banged on the door.

It flew open seconds later. "Cass!! Thank goodness you're safe! What a drama!" Tig cried.

"I know," Cass said, hugging her friend tightly. "Is Lion all right?"

"Judging by the amount of breakfast he ate he's absolutely fine," Tig replied. "He's gone off to school now. Come down to the kitchen and I'll fetch you something to eat – you must be starving," she said as they walked down the steep stairs to the kitchen. "We were expecting you days ago," Tig went on. "Did you have an awful journey?"

"Horrendous," Cass said with a grimace. "Where's Mrs Potts?"

"Upstairs resting on the sofa. You can imagine how exhausted she was after this morning," Tig said with a wry smile.

Cass and Lin giggled. "I can," Cass replied. "A lot of tea and Rimple's liqueur will be required to restore her."

"But obviously she is beside herself with excitement about you taking the Gilded Thread," Tig added. Taking the Gilded Thread was the Minarian expression for joining the queen's household. "And off on a 'diplomatic mission' as she calls it."

The three of them laughed.

"Don't ask me what Queen Arden is going to do in Bunderland," Cass said. "Because I have absolutely no idea."

"Just important queen stuff, I imagine," Tig said as she bustled around making tea and she plonked a plate of cloud cakes down on the table.

Cass sighed with pleasure. "You don't know how happy these make me. I've actually been dreaming about your cloud cakes. I have a whole week before the queen leaves and I'm not going to do anything but chat and eat cake," she announced, taking a cake and biting into the nutty sweetness.

"You must be careful on the journey, Cass," Lin said. "The news sheets have been full of talk of how bad the robbers are at the moment. I know they're based in the Forest of Thunt but apparently they've been attacking people all along the road, coming almost down to the Minarian border."

"The Sins," Cass replied with a nod. On their journey back to Minaris, Idaliz had carefully explained to Cass everything she needed to know about her duties as the queen's sword and what to watch out for on the journey into Bunderland. The main threat was to the queen's jewels, specifically from a gang of brutal thieves, known as the Sins.

"No one will get past the incredibly handsome Queen's Guard I'm sure," Tig said. "I'm so jealous of you spending a whole month with them. Let alone seeing the Ice Fair in Oskbar! It's meant to be one of the wonders of the Longest World."

Cass was about to reply but there was a loud knock on the door upstairs. "I'll go," she volunteered.

She opened the door to find a palace messenger standing there. "Miss Malvino?"

"Yes," Cass answered.

"The queen wishes to see you immediately," he announced. Cass was suddenly very aware of her dirty hair and grubby travelling clothes.

"Umm, could I just get changed and...?"

"No," the messenger replied. "You are to come this minute."

Cass sighed. "Very well." She shouted down the stairs to Tig and Lin what had happened, grabbed her cloak from the hall and followed the messenger to a waiting sledge.

As Cass walked behind the messenger along the palace's marble corridors, feeling extremely scruffy and out of place, she tried not to feel too nervous about meeting Arden. The queen was, after all, only a few years older than Cass, and Idaliz had told her repeatedly how funny and kind Arden was. Nonetheless, an unhelpful voice in Cass's head kept insisting, the queen is still the queen.

But when Cass was shown into Arden's rooms, such an amusing sight greeted her that she entirely forgot to feel nervous.

Cass found herself in a large chamber, with frescoed walls and high windows overlooking the Square of Disbelievers. But all she noticed were the towering piles of clothes, books, shoes, hats, bonnets and ribbons that covered every surface. Three vast empty trunks stood in the middle of the room, waiting to be filled for the trip. They weren't due to leave for a week but Cass supposed that packing for a queen took a long time.

Arden was standing on a high stool in the middle of the chaos, looking beautiful and hilarious, in a red silk evening dress, with her hair covered in oily mud, her face smothered in cold cream and a pair of wire-framed spectacles perched on the end of her nose. She was reading a book and eating a cinnamon cake while a dressmaker hovered around her feet, hemming the skirt she was wearing. Another woman was behind her, lacing up the back of the dress.

"Really, Tiger, I cannot breathe," Arden protested.

"Your Majesty," the woman named Tiger replied tartly. "This dress has been let out twice in the last month – you need to stop eating so many cakes!"

Cass was astounded and held her breath to see how Arden would take such a comment.

But to Cass's surprise she burst out laughing. "Honestly, you are so rude, Tiger!" Her eyes alighted on Cass. "Aha," she cried, jumping down from the stool and coming over. "Are you Cassandra, my rather late lady-in-waiting?"

As she came closer, Cass could see that Arden was indeed looking a little plumper than when she last saw her, and she was as pretty as ever under the cold cream, with her caramel-coloured skin and amused green eyes.

"Yes," Cass replied, making a deep curtsy. "But please call me Cass – everyone does. And I am so sorry to be late, we were terribly delayed by storms."

"Never mind, you are here now. But I'm afraid I've had to bring the trip forward for various reasons," Arden added vaguely. It seemed as though she would elaborate, but she only said, "So we are due to leave tomorrow. I hope that won't be too inconvenient for you."

Cass gulped a little at the thought, but replied politely, "No, of course that's fine."

"Hmm," Tiger grunted, coming towards Cass.

"It might be fine for you but it's a nightmare for me – I've got next to no time to find you some dresses and generally make you look like a lady-in-waiting, which at first glance seems a near-impossible feat."

Cass was not sure whether to laugh or be offended so she settled on no reply, only a sort of quizzical smile. Tiger was a Far Islander, around forty years old, Cass guessed, but it was hard to tell because her black skin was completely unlined. She had a strong face dominated by high, sharp cheekbones and large brown eyes. Her hair was immaculately braided, her body was slim and long-limbed and she moved like a dancer.

Tiger cast a critical eye over Cass. "Goodness me, what a state you're in – we'd better hope you scrub up well. It's hard to tell what you look like under the dirt."

Arden tutted at her and said to Cass, "This is Tiger, my chief lady-in-waiting. I do apologize for her rudeness. Now, I'm anxious that you go and see your family and rest before we set off tomorrow, so will you let the dressmaker measure you? Then we can send some Gilded Thread over to you

25

later. And please do eat some of these delicious cinnamon cakes – really, you would be doing me a favour. Tiger, please pour Cass some tea."

Tiger poured her a bowl of tea, which Cass took along with a cake and stood eating while the dressmaker measured her.

"We leave at seven o'clock tomorrow morning. You will be collected from your house at six thirty by one of my guards. Is that all clear?"

"Yes," Cass replied.

"Excellent, I look forward to getting properly acquainted on the journey. But in the meantime you must go home," Arden said.

"And have a bath," Tiger added.

"Tomorrow!" Tig exclaimed when Cass got home.

"I know," Cass said with a sigh. She felt exhausted. "I can't face going out again to the bathhouse – will you help me have a bath in the copper?" she asked.

"Of course," Tig replied and together they boiled enough water to fill the large copper washing basin in the basement kitchen. As Cass got undressed,

Tig said, "And you'd better give me your citizen necklace to polish up as well, so you look like a proper Minarian."

"Thanks," Cass replied, unhooking the gold necklace from her neck. The fish charm dangled from, it showing that she was a free citizen of the city. "Do you mind cleaning my ring too?" she asked, to which Tig replied of course not. The ring had been a present from Lin when Cass had set off on her adventure the year before, and it had allowed Lin to keep an eye on Cass.

Cass lowered herself into the warm water with a sigh of pleasure that almost instantly turned to a yelp of horror as the water turned a soupy grey.

"That's revolting!" she cried. "I must be absolutely filthy."

"I'd better put some more hot water on," Tig responded with a laugh.

The rest of the afternoon slipped away. Lion returned home from school and seemed in perfect health and as jolly as ever. Mrs Potts raised herself from her sofa just in time to shriek with delight

27

over the trunk that was delivered from the palace.

It was navy-blue leather with the queen's coronet embossed on the lid and when opened it revealed a perfectly packed trunk containing two day dresses in a heavy navy fabric shot through with gold, one evening dress in gold-and-navy silk and a navy sheepskin coat with gold fastenings. There were also boots, indoor shoes (all in embroidered bags), white underdresses, camisoles and pantaloons, as well as hairbrushes, and a box full of glass bottles and pots of various lotions and creams, which Cass was unsure what she was supposed to do with.

"My Cassandra, taking the Gilded Thread," Mrs Potts said with a contented sigh. "I still cannot quite believe it. Mind you, dear, it's a shame you're going so soon," she added, in case Cass thought her heartless.

They ate a hasty tea of oyster stew and crackleberry tart, while Mrs Potts filled Cass in on all the square gossip. Then Cass nipped over to see Lin before her friend was inundated with customers wanting their fortunes told.

"You're going tomorrow?!" Lin said.

Cass nodded. "I know; it's such a rush."

"Never mind. You'll be back before you know it, and please write! Tell me all about the amazing things you see," Lin said, giving her a hug.

"I will," Cass replied. "And I'll see you at the Mid-Winter Feast!"

"Absolutely. Oh, you must go on a sledshot in Oskbar."

"What's a sledshot?" Cass asked, intrigued.

"Wait and see," Lin replied with a laugh.

An hour later, the night district of Minaris was in full swing, and the Mansion of Fortune had a long queue of clients waiting to see the fortune tellers and trancers that Mrs Potts crammed into the rooms. Tig and Lion were busy organizing it all. Although Cass had begun to help, Tig told her very firmly to go to bed.

Cass could hardly stand she was so exhausted and gratefully accepted. She made her way to the tiny room in the basement that she was sharing with Lion for the night – Mrs Potts had wasted no time in letting out her room to a trancer – gave her teeth a quick clean and set her old alarm clock for six.

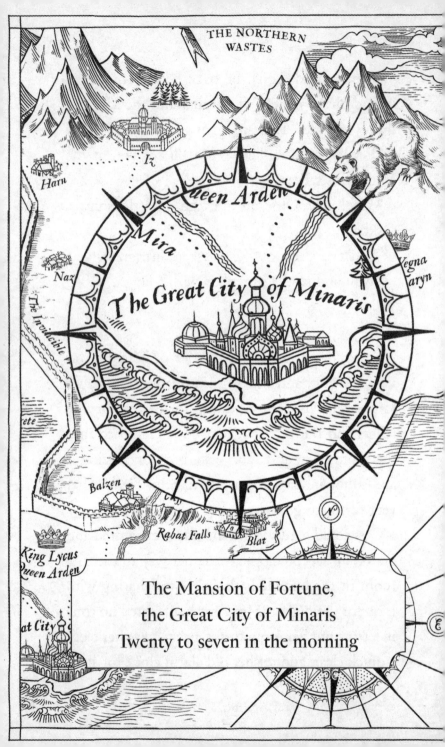

THE NORTHERN
WASTES

Harn

Iz

Queen Arden

Mira

Naz

The Invincible

Vegna
Caryn

The Great City of Minaris

ete

Balzen

Rabat Falls

Blat

King Lycus
Queen Arden

at City

The Mansion of Fortune,
the Great City of Minaris
Twenty to seven in the morning

N

3

The Queen's Sword

Cass was dreaming.

She was back in the Islands chasing a pirate named Zirt. He had always stood apart from the others – he wasn't a disgruntled, penniless Far Islander but a pale-skinned, well fed northerner who had joined the pirates relatively recently. He was part of a gang that Cass, Rip and the Company of Eight had pursued across the Mid Isles, finally tracking them down in an inn in the night district of Tarn and ambushing them.

Zirt always seemed to seek Cass out, she had noticed, taunting her and calling her 'kitten'. And there was something about the way he fought that she found particularly difficult. Their final battle, for that was what it felt like, took every ounce of Cass's skill and strength. She had eventually triumphed and Zirt had been captured and taken to Prison Island along with the others. But the fight still haunted her.

In the dream, Cass's mind replayed the end of the scene. She had fenced Zirt up against the alley wall, knocked the sword out of his hand and held her blade to his throat. Their faces were inches from each other and she took in his widely spaced blue eyes and large nose, the scar on his cheek, his fair skin burnt to a ruddy gold by the sun. In real life, he had then sworn and spat at her, but in the dream, he pulled a dagger from somewhere and plunged it into Cass's side, making her wake up with a jolt, sweating and disorientated. There was a terrible noise and it took her a second to realize that someone was hammering on the front door.

Who in the Longest World can that be? she wondered, swinging herself out of bed. She glanced at Lion who was lying flat on his back, snoring loudly, his arms and legs stretched out like a starfish. *I wonder what time it is?* she thought, noticing that it was just getting light outside. She glanced at the alarm clock and saw that it read one o'clock. *That can't be right…* Her stomach plummeted as she realized that the clock must have stopped. *Bang! Bang!* The noise came again. Cass dashed upstairs to open the front door.

A young man dressed in the Queen's Guard uniform was standing there, looking furious.

"Cassandra?" he demanded angrily. "I've been knocking for ten minutes. Weren't you told to expect me?"

"Yes," Cass said. "I'm really sorry. My alarm clock must be broken and—"

"The queen leaves in fifteen minutes," he interrupted her brusquely. "It will take us ten minutes to get back to the palace so unless you want to keep her waiting, which I really wouldn't advise, you'd better go and get dressed. Be back here in three minutes. Do you need help?"

"Er, no. I'll just go and—"

"Hurry," he instructed.

Cass flew back down the stairs and dressed as quickly as she could, pulling apart the neatly packed trunk. There was no time to say goodbye

33

to anyone and Lion looked so peaceful snoring that she just kissed his head while trying to lace up her boots and do up her dress. It was fiendishly intricate with lots of small buttons. And the coat seemed complicated too…

The young man appeared in the doorway.

"Come on!" he said and they carried the trunk up the stairs and loaded it on to the back of the sledge.

"Ready?" he asked Cass as they both scrambled up on to the broad driving seat.

"Yes," she replied but just as he started to drive off she remembered her knife and sword.

"Sorry, I've forgotten something really important!" she cried. The guardsman groaned and swore under his breath as he stopped the sledge. Cass jumped down and ran back to her room, grabbing her weapons, her purse and various other things she had forgotten. She shoved the knife and purse in her pocket and wrapped the rest in a blanket to hide the sword.

"I'm so glad you went back for your blanket," the guardsman said sarcastically as Cass put it in the trunk. "We're always short of such things with the queen."

The sledge sped through the empty streets as Cass hurriedly finished doing up her boots and her coat. The young man glanced at her. "You might want to do something about your hair. Ladies-in-waiting usually look quite neat," he said, a smile breaking through his aggravation. Cass put her hands up to her head and could feel that her hair, now clean and washed, had turned into a mass of springy curls on the top of her head.

"Oh no!" she cried as the sledge swung around in front of the palace and she desperately tried to smooth it down.

Queen Arden was only travelling with a small party but nevertheless it was still quite a spectacle. It had snowed overnight, giving the ground and buildings a sprinkling of pristine white, making them the perfect backdrop for the queen's two navy-blue and gilt carriage sledges, which were drawn by four white horses each. Around them stood the other nine members of the Queen's Guard, looking splendid in their blue-and-gold riding uniforms, their horses stamping and snorting in the cold. Their breath came out like smoke, giving them the look of fairy-tale creatures.

"Where have you been?" a middle-aged man barked at them as the sledge came to a halt. *This must be Captain Toskil,* Cass thought, judging by the amount of gold on his uniform. Idaliz had told her that he was a good man, if a little severe. Cass braced herself for a telling-off.

"I'm very sorry, Captain," the guardsman replied. "I was late collecting the young lady. I had to stop to help an elderly gentleman who was in some distress – he had locked himself out of his house."

Cass thought grateful thoughts, keeping her face neutral.

"I see. Captain Toskil, by the way," he said, bowing to her.

"Cassandra Malvino," she replied, bowing back. His looked at her with interest. He was one of the few people who would know that she was really there as the queen's sword.

"Well, Cassandra," the captain went on. "You'd better go and wait by the queen's sledge. Guardsman, get this trunk loaded up and then go and wait with Miss Malvino so that you can help the queen when she comes out." And beating his whip gently on his leg, he walked away.

"Thank you," Cass whispered to the young man.

"Don't worry about it, Miss Malvino," he replied.

"You must call me Cass. What's your name?" she asked.

"Dacha," he replied as another guard came to help him carry Cass's trunk to the luggage sledge.

Dacha, was that a Bundish or a Veraklian name? Cass mused as they waited on either side of the queen's sledge as instructed. Veraklian, she decided, was more likely with his brown eyes and coppery hair. Veraklia was the country to the north-east of Minaris. It'd had a lot of difficulties in recent years and many of its citizens had emigrated to Minaris.

The first person to emerge from the palace was Tiger, looking immaculate in her Gilded Thread and carrying Arden's jewel case. A palace servant scurried behind her holding a pile of navy-blue document boxes that were loaded inside the sledge.

"Good morning," she greeted the captain. "The queen's latest thoughts are that we will just stop briefly at Perla at midday to change the horses, and then as long as the snow holds off we will press on to Aravura. She is anxious to reach there tonight. She will be out in a moment and wants to leave immediately, so said for you all to mount."

Orders were barked and Dacha helped Tiger into the sledge. She wished him and Cass a brisk good morning and Cass could feel her eyes lingering disapprovingly over her hair. Cass tried to pat it down even further, to Dacha's discreet amusement. Moments later, there was a flurry of activity by the palace door and Arden appeared, dressed in honey-coloured fur.

"Good morning, everyone!" she cried cheerfully, walking over to her sledge. There was a chorus of polite replies and Dacha opened the door of the sledge for her, bowing low.

"Good morning, Dacha. How are you?" Arden asked him.

"Very well, Your Majesty, thank you," he replied.

"Good morning, Cass," Arden said as Cass curtsied to her. "Have you two met?" she asked as Dacha helped her into the sledge.

"I had the honour of collecting Miss Malvino

from her house this morning," he replied, with just a faint touch of laughter around his eyes and in his voice.

"Excellent," Arden replied, smiling. She sensed a joke but she didn't pursue it. "Well, I am very lucky to have her, Dacha, so you be sure to be kind to her and give her any help she needs. Not that I think she'll need any; she is a most capable young lady by all accounts."

"I'm sure that's true, Your Majesty," Dacha replied smoothly. And after Cass had got into the sledge, he closed the door behind them.

The sledge was quite the most luxurious that Cass had ever seen, with velvet-covered seats more comfortable than armchairs, and a burner which meant that it was as toasty as Mrs Potts's overheated little parlour. There were even candles in holders which Tiger lit and Arden immediately opened the first of the navy-blue boxes that had been placed by her seat. She pulled a pair of spectacles from her pocket and began to read the stack of papers within them. Tiger fussed around arranging things, and then she got some embroidery out of a basket that had been placed on the floor of the carriage. Cass felt rather at a loss without anything to do.

"Can you sew, Cass?" Tiger asked her abruptly.

"Er, yes, but not brilliantly," Cass replied, feeling inadequate.

Tiger began to rootle around in the basket, but Arden said, looking up from her documents, "Let her sleep, Tiger. Cass, you still look shattered. While we are in the Minarian outlands, why don't you rest? Don't worry, you're not here for your sewing skills. The mending can wait."

Cass thanked her and by the time they passed through the city gates, her eyelids were drooping and soon the warmth of the sledge and the rocking movement had lulled her into a heavy sleep.

Cass was indeed exhausted and slept for most of the day. This time her sleep was untroubled and she did not wake up until late in the afternoon. She rubbed her eyes a little and looked out of the window to see that the day had been and gone and the sky was dark. She could only dimly pick out the silhouettes of the guards riding beside them. Arden looked up from her papers, noticing Cass was awake.

"Better?" she asked.

"Much," Cass replied, stretching her neck. It was stiff from being in the same position for hours.

"Good. You must be starving," Arden remarked and without waiting for a response said, "Tiger, hand Cass the tiffin box and please pour her some tea. You must have one of these excellent scoodle pies."

Tiger put down her sewing and did as Arden had instructed. Cass drank the cup of bitter tea gratefully as she was thirsty and helped herself to one of the scoodle pies, which were indeed very fine – flaky and cheesy in just the right amount.

"Aren't they delicious?" Arden asked. "Cass, you'll have to forgive me. I adore feeding people. You must tell me if it becomes annoying!"

Cass laughed, replying, "I love food so I can't imagine it will. And they are very tasty scoodle pies." She glanced back out of the window as she cleaned her hands on a napkin that Tiger passed her. "Where are we?" she asked.

"We'll be at Aravura soon," Arden replied.

Sure enough, about fifteen minutes later street lanterns appeared, casting an orange light that

41

illuminated the outskirts of a town.

The pretty border town of Aravura sat at the confluence of two rivers and was famous for the ancient stone bridges that spanned them. It had long been at the centre of trade between the Bundish and Minarians. In the summer the water was crowded with barges and in winter, when the rivers froze, they became like roads, alive with skaters and sledges. As the royal party arrived, people turned and cheered and Arden stuck her head out of the window, waving at everyone.

"I do like this inn," Arden remarked as the sledges drew up in front of a large stone building. It looked inviting with every window brightly lit. The Inn of the Leaping Fish, Cass read on the sign. "The beds are particularly comfortable and the landlady is a sweetie. Remind me, Tiger, is the mayor coming to me for dinner?"

Tiger nodded. "With his wife and eldest daughter."

The sledge had hardly stopped when the door shot open and a lady appeared, her face eager and shiny with excitement. She scurried over to the sledge and opened the door before any of the

42

Queen's Guard were off their horses.

"Your Majesty, we have been so excited about your visit," she cried, bobbing up and down in a curtsy. "Here, let me help you down. I have cooked all your favourite dishes and the water is heated ready for your bath."

"Thank you so much," Arden replied. "It is indeed nice to be back here. Now, tell me, how are your children? Your son had a terrible cough the last time I came and we left you with a bottle of Tiger's special linctus…" Taking the landlady's arm she walked up to the inn, while behind her a scene of organized chaos unfolded, as stable boys ran to take the horses and the inn staff rushed around, unloading trunks and taking orders from Captain Toskil.

Meanwhile, Cass, mindful of her real role on the journey, had a good look at the inn. There was the main building in front, with the stables on the left and a separate guesthouse to the right, which was where they would be staying. It sat right by the river and Cass was just wondering if there was a path between the river and the house when her thoughts were interrupted.

"You go with the queen, Cass. I'll sort out the luggage," Tiger instructed.

Cass followed Arden and the landlady through the front door of the guesthouse and into the cosy hall.

"You'll remember I'm sure that the receiving rooms are to the right, and that is where we'll show the mayor to when he arrives in an hour or so," the landlady was saying to Arden. "Then on the left are the kitchens and quarters for your guardsmen. Now, let me take you up to your rooms." They walked up the stairs. "Here is your bedchamber, Your Majesty, and then there are two smaller rooms for your ladies-in-waiting. I hope that's satisfactory."

"This all looks perfect, thank you. Now, if you'll excuse me I will get ready." Arden dismissed the landlady with a smile. "Cass, please can you help me with my things."

"Yes, of course." Cass hurried over.

"Gloves first," Arden instructed, holding her hands out to Cass, who pulled the gloves off as delicately as she could.

"Hat next," she said and Cass removed the fur

44

hat. "And now my coat." It was fastened with a single button, which was easy enough for Cass to undo, but she could still feel her hands quivering with nerves.

"Hang them up over there," Tiger said, coming into the room and pointing to a set of hooks and hangers on one wall. "Carefully," she added.

"Tiger," Arden said. "I'm going to have a bath and then get ready for the mayor. Is my travelling trunk on its way in?"

"It's just coming now. Are you still happy to wear the green silk tonight?"

"Yes," Arden replied. "Cass, can you help me off with my boots, please." Cass knelt down and untied her laces then eased them off her feet.

A procession of servants brought in one of the queen's enormous trunks and Cass and Tiger's much smaller ones. "Put the large trunk there, please, and then the other ones, put one in each room. Cass, the jewel case always goes by the queen's bed. Do not move it under any circumstances," Tiger instructed. "Now, please can you go downstairs and find the maids. Tell them to bring the copper and hot water up for the queen's bath and we also need an iron. Not too hot but hot enough. It's for silk."

"Of course," Cass replied, feeling slightly overwhelmed.

"And some lavender tea too, please, Cass," Arden called after her.

Cass dashed down to the kitchens and found the maids, who were a great deal surlier than their mistress. However, she chivvied them along, and the copper, hot water and iron were brought upstairs. But the iron proved too cold, the water too hot and where was the lavender tea? Up and down the stairs Cass ran, chasing forgotten soap, fetching more tea, more cold water, until at last Arden, looking every inch the queen in a magnificent ruby necklace and earrings and an emerald-green silk evening dress, walked graciously down the stairs to greet the mayor.

With a sigh of relief, Cass set about helping Tiger clear up the muddle that Arden had left behind. The room was stuffy with heat and perfume, so Cass eased open one of the casement windows to let some air in. As she glanced down to the river path she gave a start, because she clearly saw a figure loitering there. They immediately stepped back into the shadows, obviously having seen her at the window. She remembered the warning Idaliz had given her before they parted. "Do not get complacent at any point on the journey; you will be being watched. The queen's jewels are like a magnet to the Sins and other thieves."

A maid appeared with a tray laden with bowls of pumpkin soup for Tiger and Cass, accompanied by a loaf of soft white bread and two generous helpings of rambleberry tart and cream.

"Mmm," Tiger said appreciatively. "Let's eat this before it gets cold."

But Cass was pulling on her coat. "You go ahead, I just need to check something," she said, hurrying out of the room, leaving a bewildered Tiger.

"Just getting a breath of air," she said to the guards by the main door, before sprinting round to the back of the house.

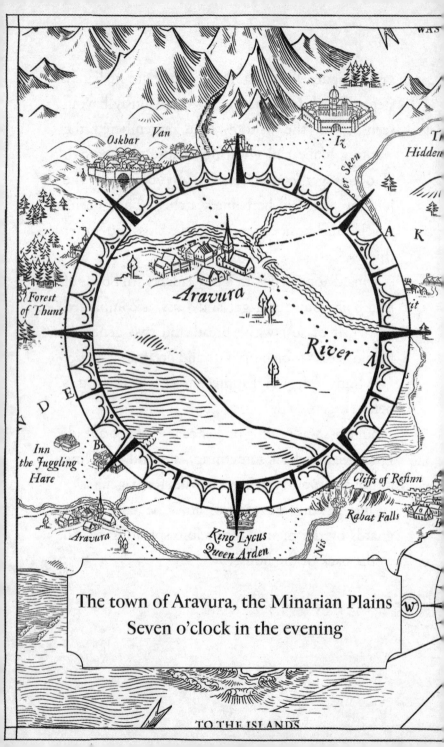

The town of Aravura, the Minarian Plains
Seven o'clock in the evening

4

Unexpected Visitors

The moon's white light reflected back off the river and the snow, which meant that Cass could see pretty well. There was a line of trees between the path and river and, as Cass walked along, a small figure shot out from behind one of them, sprinting away from her. Cass could see it was a child and she sped after them. They were quick but Cass was faster, so it only took her a moment to catch them.

It was a young girl of about ten dressed in a hotchpotch of grubby furs with a grimy, frightened face. *A scared child*, Cass thought, relaxing, although she still asked her, "What were you doing lurking there?"

"I wanted to see the queen," the girl replied in a sing-song voice. "Is it true that she's staying in the inn and is on her way to Oskbar?"

"Perhaps," Cass said with a smile.

"Are you one of her ladies-in-waiting?"

"Yes," Cass replied.

The child began to sing a well-known nursery rhyme,

"Oh, I'm the Queen of Minaris

And all the ladies have to curtsy to me,

Curtsy to me,

Curtsy to me,

In the City of the Fishshhhhhhh."

And as she drew out the *shh* of *fish* she raised one finger up to her mouth, as if she was telling Cass to be quiet.

"Very good." Cass applauded her.

"You're very pretty," the girl went on. "Are you from Minaris?"

"Yes," Cass replied.

"What's your name?"

"Cass. Now I've got a question for you. Have you eaten tonight?"

The girl shook her head. Cass pulled a silver

out of her pocket and pressed it into the girl's hand. "Go and get some food. No more skulking around." The girl, looking delighted by the money, skipped off.

Cass went back upstairs and ate supper with Tiger, and then wrote brief letters to Rip, Mrs Potts and Tig. She kept a watch out of the window but there was no sign of anyone else down by the river. However, Idaliz's instructions were firmly anchored in her mind and since Arden was expected to be occupied with the mayor for another hour at least, she decided to take the letters up to the main inn to post and take a look around.

She saw nothing unusual until she was about to head back to the guesthouse, when she noticed the young girl from before. She was speaking to a man, a northerner around thirty years old, with dark hair and eyes, dressed in a scruffy, nondescript way. He listened intently to what she said then handed her some coins.

Cass was alarmed. Perhaps the girl had been spying after all. The girl slipped away and the man headed upstairs to his room. Cass waited to see if he would reappear but there was no further sign of him so she returned to the queen's quarters. She helped Tiger get Arden to bed, all the time wondering uneasily about the man and the girl and the silvers that had passed between them. When Cass finally got to bed herself, she found that no matter how much she told herself the queen was safe with guards posted outside her door and several more downstairs, her brain would not settle and she slept poorly, waking every hour or so to check on Arden.

The following day dawned cold and clear. The sky was bright blue and it had snowed lightly overnight, making everything glitter and dance like diamonds in the sharp sunshine. The sparkling weather lifted Cass's spirits, and although she was still wary, she decided that she had been overly suspicious the night before and it was probably nothing.

The sledges were ushered through the border crossing without delay and when they were only a little way into Bunderland, Cass, her eyes moving restlessly around, noticed that the scenery began to change from the flat Minarian Plains. The road rose and fell as gentle slopes appeared in the white landscape and orchards broke up the monotony of fields. Groups of cottages appeared, with diamond-paned windows and deep-thatched roofs. Trails of smoke escaped from the chimneys and the yards were full of geese, chickens, goats and cows. The frozen River Mira meandered along next to them, crowded with sledges and skaters wearing traditional Bundish embroidered sheepskin coats and hats. They saw the royal sledge and waved and cheered.

"The people here seem happy," Cass remarked to Arden.

"I think they are," she replied. "Everyone has enough food to eat and extra to sell on to earn some silvers; we are on the fringes of the fertile lands of Metrete."

"Ah, yes," Cass replied, remembering her geography from school. "Metrete was part of Veraklia before the Magical Wars, wasn't it?"

Arden nodded. "It was taken from them by the Bundish as compensation for Veraklia starting the wars. But looking back I'm not sure it was the right thing to do. Not only does Veraklia still miss Metrete terribly in terms of feeding the rest of the country, it also hurt their pride, making them turn in on themselves. You have to remember, Cass, that Veraklia was once the richest and most powerful nation in the Longest World and then suddenly they were struggling to feed their people. It was soon afterwards that they started to build the Invincible Wall and the country has become more and more closed with every year, until we have the situation now where the borders are entirely shut and even messenger birds are shot down."

Cass nodded, wondering whether Arden would mention Idaliz. The reason Cass had taken Idaliz's place as Arden's sword was that King Lycus had sent Idaliz to Veraklia to try and find out what was going on there. Idaliz was Veraklian herself and therefore able to blend in to a certain degree, but it was still incredibly dangerous. The country was ruled by the tyrannical Queen Vegna. Her informers were everywhere and anyone suspected of spying for a foreign government would be instantly put to death. Cass felt anxious for Idaliz whenever she thought about it.

Arden looked as if she were about to say something else but thought better of it. The conversation moved on and although Cass listened far more than she contributed, partly because she was keeping her eyes on their surroundings, she enjoyed herself. Arden and Tiger were good company, both fiercely intelligent and well read, and it was interesting to listen to them debating politics or discussing books.

At about midday, with an air of secrecy, the sledges turned off the main road and slithered on to a track that led quickly into a dense forest. Cass was surprised and must have looked it, for Arden, after exchanging glances with Tiger, said, "Cass, we are going to meet someone. She is an old friend of mine and I need to know I can rely on your discretion."

"Of course," Cass replied, trying to look as nonchalant as possible, although inside she was alive with curiosity. What old friend could Arden have that she couldn't meet in the open?

After about ten minutes, the coaches stopped. Captain Toskil dismounted and appeared by the sledge window.

"The cabin is over there, Your Majesty," he said, pointing to a narrow path through the snow. Cass could see a small, simple wooden hut, almost hidden among the trees just a few minutes' walk away. "I don't believe the other party has arrived yet."

"Very good," Arden replied. "Cass, as my sword, you'd better come with me and I'll take Dacha too. Captain, please will you stay here to put off anyone who should happen to come along the lane."

"Very well, Your Majesty," Captain Toskil agreed.

Cass quickly checked that her knife was in her pocket. It was a spring knife that folded up small enough to fit in the pocket of her dress.

She had hidden her sword under a blanket in the carriage and she wondered for a moment whether she should bring it. Arden, reading her mind, said, "No swords, Cass. It wouldn't be appropriate."

As they got out of the sledge, Captain Toskil was giving orders. "Dacha, go and check the cabin first."

Dacha jumped neatly down from his horse and jogged along the path to the cabin. Cass scanned the wood. It appeared empty but it was hard to tell with so many trees. Arden picked up her skirt and walked along the path to the cabin, with Cass following closely behind.

"All clear," Dacha announced as he came out.

"Would you like me to light you a fire in there, Your Majesty?"

Arden shook her head. "No, the less attention we draw the better." As she finished speaking they all heard the gentle thud of hooves in the snow. "Here she comes," Arden said.

Dacha and Cass looked away discreetly as a young woman on horseback rode up. In the black-and-white winter landscape, her rust-coloured furs and copper hair were as vivid as jewels.

Who is she? Cass speculated as Dacha bowed deeply to the young woman and then helped her off the horse. Cass followed his lead and bowed too.

The young woman nodded at them and curtsied graciously to Arden. "Thank you so much for agreeing to meet me, Your Majesty."

"It's my pleasure. Now, come inside so we can talk. Dacha will look after your horse."

The pair disappeared into the cabin, shutting the door firmly behind them.

Cass looked at Dacha quizzically.

"Princess Taryn," he mouthed back at her.

"No!" Cass couldn't stop herself exclaiming.

Taryn was the niece of Vegna, the Veraklian

queen. Taryn's father had been king until he and his wife had tragically been killed in a sledging accident, when Taryn was a baby. Her aunt Vegna had ruled in her place. Taryn was due to come of age shortly and inherit the throne, but a few months ago she had disappeared. There had been all sorts of wild rumours about her living wild in the Northern Wastes or even being murdered by Queen Vegna.

"I'm as surprised as you," Dacha said. "I would never have guessed that she would be in Bunderland. The news sheets said that she had fled to the Islands."

Cass nodded in response, absorbing the information. But then there was a rustling, a noise on the roof. They both jumped and reached for their weapons. But it was only a small blue bird.

"A woodland warbler," Dacha said, sounding pleased.

"Aren't they supposed to be lucky?" Cass asked

"They are indeed," he replied, just as the cabin door opened and the two women came out.

Dacha and Cass looked at the ground as Taryn said, "I can't thank you enough, Arden."

"I cannot promise anything," Arden responded. "But I think the Bundish will be as alarmed as I am by what you have told me and I will do my best to persuade King Hoff to help. You know you have Minaris's support at any rate, whatever you decide to do. Are you safe where you are? You can always come to the Minarian court."

"It's kind of you but I think it's better I stay hidden for the time being. For me to be at the Minarian court would only enrage my aunt further."

Arden nodded and they said goodbye to each other. Taryn rode off and Arden, Dacha and Cass walked back to their sledge in silence. Cass noticed that Arden looked worried, and she spent the afternoon staring out of the window and scribbling a letter to King Lycus, which she sent back to Minaris with one of the guard immediately.

They spent the night in the town of Baden at the Inn of Few Surprises, which to Cass's relief lived up to its name. She slipped out again in the evening to see if she could see the man from Aravura but there was no sign of him. Perhaps it had been nothing, Cass tried to reassure herself so that she might get a good night's sleep.

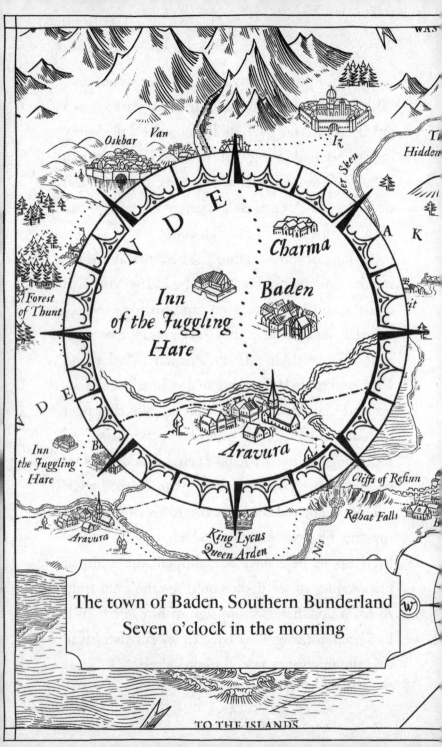

The town of Baden, Southern Bunderland
Seven o'clock in the morning

5

The Inn of the Juggling Hare

They woke up in Baden to another fine day and set off early, stopping briefly to change horses at lunchtime at an inn in Jena. It was then that Cass caught sight of the dark-haired man again. He was hanging around the stables and she saw him strike up a conversation with one of the Queen's Guard. Cass walked over there but by the time she reached them, he had gone.

"What was that man asking you about?" she asked the guard.

"Nothing," the guard replied with a shrug. "Just making conversation about the horses."

The sledges left soon afterwards and Cass turned

the incident over in her mind. Perhaps it was entirely innocent; the man was merely another traveller on the road through Bunderland. Maybe he had spoken to the girl in Aravura, just as Cass had, and had also felt sorry for her and given her some coins. Then he happened to be at the inn just now, stabling his horses and had casually struck up a conversation with the guard. It all made perfect logical sense, and yet it wouldn't quite sit with Cass.

As the afternoon waned a bank of cloud appeared from the north and the air cooled. "Oh, drat! Here comes snow," Arden exclaimed as the first few fat flakes twirled out of the sky.

"It always starts mildly," Tiger remarked. "And before you know it you're stuck in a drift as high as a child."

"Oh, don't say that!" Arden cried. "I'm desperate to reach Charma tonight, otherwise it will mess everything up. We have a long enough journey tomorrow to reach Darn by nightfall, and then another long day travelling through the Forest of Thunt."

But Tiger was right. Before half an hour had

passed the snow was pouring from the sky. They pressed on but it wasn't long before Captain Toskil stopped them and appeared at the window of their sledge.

"I'm sorry, Your Majesty, we're not going to make it to Charma. I suggest we take shelter in the nearest inn. I believe there is one not much further along the road."

"Very well," Arden replied with a sigh. "You'd better send a guard ahead to warn them."

The Juggling Hare was not the usual type of coaching inn Arden would stop at – it was rather more ... rough and ready. There was nothing wrong with that in itself, Cass thought, but the rooms set aside for the queen were bound to be less secure and the clientele more likely to notice their arrival. And indeed the landlord was a large burly man, clearly more used to chucking drunks out of his inn than welcoming a queen. But he endeared himself to Cass by being as delighted as a child by Arden's arrival.

He welcomed her into the inn, apologizing

for its lack of an annex. "But the top floor has some fine rooms," he explained, "which are being readied for you at this moment, Your Majesty. Would you allow me to escort you there?"

Cass walked just behind Arden and enjoyed the looks of disbelief on the faces of everyone in the inn as Arden strolled elegantly across the filthy floor, wishing them all a good evening. Cass glanced around and could see no sign of the dark-haired man, but her heart nevertheless sank a little. *Everyone in there looked like they could be a member of the Sins,* she thought with grim amusement.

The rooms comprised two connecting chambers, one for Arden and the other for Cass and Tiger. They had balconies – easy access for a thief, Cass noted with irritation. Captain Toskil and the rest of the guard were accommodated in the other rooms on the floor, which all gave on to a central corridor.

Cass and Tiger settled Arden by the fire and set about making the rooms rather more fit for a queen. Arden travelled with a set of her own linen, so they remade the bed using it. Cass found a mop and cleaned the floor properly, while Tiger located a basin and a jug of hot water so that Arden could at least wash. Much to everyone's surprise, the supper, when it arrived, was delicious. A rabbit stew flavoured with herbs and good crusty bread and apple tart with thick cream.

Arden was exhausted so she went straight to bed and Tiger soon followed. Cass decided against going downstairs to the bar, as she would be too conspicuous. Instead she spent some time on her balcony, which looked out on to the forecourt, watching for anything unusual. But it was still snowing hard and there was nothing to see, so she came back inside, locking the door behind her. She double-checked that there were guards posted outside the doors and then decided there was nothing for it but to go to bed.

It must have been about two o'clock in the morning when something disturbed Cass. Instantly she was awake. There was someone in the room, she could sense it, but she forced herself to keep her breathing regular as she opened her eyes the tiniest bit. Although the room was dark she could see the silhouette of a man, standing in the doorway to the balcony. He appeared to be getting something out of his pocket.

Reaching under the bed for her sword, Cass leaped up. The movement startled the man and he immediately ran back on to the balcony, and before Cass could stop him he clambered over it. Cass ran to the edge to see him scramble down a rope and land next to a horse and rider. The rider pulled him up on to his horse and they galloped off before Cass could even get her leg over the balcony to follow.

Swearing to herself, she darted back inside to check on Arden. The connecting door was shut but Cass opened it gently and tiptoed inside. To Cass's immense relief, Arden was in bed asleep, breathing normally and her jewel case was sitting undisturbed by her bed. Cass quietly shut the door and, after putting her sword back under her bed and swapping her nightgown for a dress, she went out to the main corridor.

Dacha and another guard were sitting outside. "The queen is fine but there was a man, an intruder, in our bedroom," she announced to them. Alarmed, they scrambled to their feet.

"I disturbed him and he jumped down off the balcony. He had an accomplice waiting for him and they rode off together. They're long gone now – there's no point trying to follow him," Cass explained matter-of-factly.

"You seem very calm about it," Dacha remarked, looking at Cass curiously as they followed her back into the room. He still had no idea that she was the queen's sword.

"What's going on?" Tiger asked, waking up.

"There was a man in our room. He came in from the balcony," Cass explained, going back to the balcony door. The lock had been sprung.

Tiger gasped, immediately saying, "The queen! Is she all right?"

"She's fine," Cass replied. "I've already checked."

"And her jewels?"

"Still there," Cass confirmed.

Dacha went out on to the balcony, treading on something that looked like a handkerchief. It crunched under his feet and there was an incredibly strong smell of spirits. He jumped back into the room and they all backed away, putting their hands up to cover their noses and mouths and shut the door.

"What in the Longest World is that?" the other guard asked.

"It smells like etherine," Cass said. "I think you just trod on one of the intruder's etherine balls."

"What are etherine balls?" Tiger asked.

"They are mostly used as party tricks to make someone faint for a few minutes. You can buy them in the night market in Minaris," Cass explained.

"Do you think they were going to abduct the queen?" Tiger asked, sounding very alarmed. Cass was thinking the same thing.

"Not necessarily," Dacha replied. "Robbers often use them to deepen a person's sleep. We must tell Captain Toskil," he said to the other guard.

The captain appeared, looking grim. More of the guard were woken and told to patrol outside. Then he asked Cass to accompany him to his room and, once he'd shut the door, said, "The Sins presumably? After the queen's jewels?"

"I would guess so," she replied. "There were two

of them and they had covered their faces. I'm sorry I can't really tell you any more than that."

He paused, chewing his lip anxiously as he considered the situation. "You haven't noticed anything else, have you, to indicate we're being followed?"

Cass weighed up in her mind whether to tell Captain Toskil about the dark-haired man and decided that she should. "It is probably nothing," she began and then told the captain about seeing the man in Aravura handing money to the girl and then seeing him again at lunchtime.

The captain listened carefully and then gave a slight shrug. "As you say, it's probably nothing but it's good you're keeping such a close eye on matters. We have no option but to continue and just be as vigilant as possible."

The conversation finished and Cass went back to her bed. Tiger was back under her blankets. Cass couldn't tell if she was asleep or not, but she was silent at any rate. Cass tried to sleep but she was too nervous and wide awake, so she lay staring at the ceiling instead until it was time to get up.

Breakfast was a subdued affair. The snow had ceased leaving a cheerless cold grey day. Everyone was keen to leave the inn as soon as possible. Arden had been told of the intruder and had taken the news calmly.

"However, I think it would be sensible to ask my cousin Maer to send additional guards to escort us through the Forest of Thunt – do you agree?" she said to Captain Toskil.

Cass could see the captain was slightly offended by this suggestion but he replied evenly, "Whatever Your Majesty thinks best."

Arden gave a small nod and after a moment's consideration replied, "Yes, I do think it would be best. Will you send one of the guard ahead, Captain, to the next town and send a bird. The men should meet us at the inn at Danske either tonight or at first light tomorrow morning."

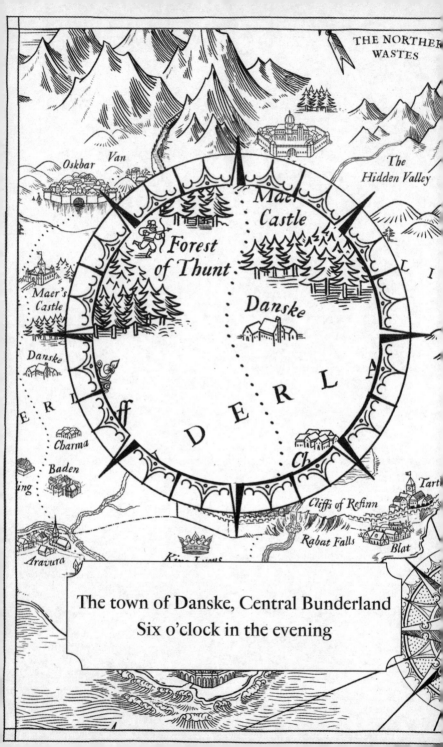

The town of Danske, Central Bunderland
Six o'clock in the evening

6

The Sins

They travelled all day, reaching Danske in the early evening. The town lay on the fringes of the Forest of Thunt and the inn they were staying in was on a pretty cobbled square near its centre. It was a well run, comfortable sort of place, and Cass was relieved to find that the royal party was staying in a separate house. She cast her eye over the building. No balconies, just sheer walls and casement windows with shallow sills and a single staircase up and down. *Infinitely easier to defend,* she thought, her mood lightening. As the landlady was showing them around, the extra men arrived, easing her mind even further.

Nevertheless, after Cass had helped Tiger get Arden ready for a dinner with a couple of local dignitaries, she decided she should go and just have a quick look around. Using letters as an excuse again she went downstairs. Dacha was in the hall, standing with a couple of other guards.

"Off out?" he asked Cass.

"Yes." She held up the letters. "I'm just going to the postage office."

"I'll come with you," he said.

"No, really, I'll be fine," Cass protested. That was the last thing she wanted.

"I insist," Dacha replied. "Captain Toskil would roast me alive if he knew that I'd let you go off on your own."

He wouldn't, Cass thought but she decided it was easier to agree.

They made their way across the square and down one of the side alleys, following signs to the postage office. Dacha walked beside Cass, his hands shoved deep in his pockets, telling her a series of funny stories while she surreptitiously glanced around. And although it was bitterly cold, it felt good to be out in the fresh air after being cooped up in the stuffy sledge and overheated inn.

They turned into a street, which was unexpectedly full of people. Cass noticed the signs for fortune telling and trancing. "This must be the town's night district," she remarked to Dacha but he didn't answer. His gaze was fixed on the sky. Cass looked around and saw that so too was everyone else's.

Sighing a little, she asked Dacha, "What can you see up there?"

He looked at her in amazement.

"I'm an obtuse," she explained.

"No!" he exclaimed. "Really? I've never met an obtuse before."

"We're a rare breed," Cass replied breezily. "So what am I missing?"

"The sky is full of golden butterflies," he said. "And, oh yes, they are just arranging themselves into the words Free Magic!"

As he said that, the crowd began to chant, "Free Magic! Free Magic!"

"Come on, we need to get out of here before the enforcers turn up and there's trouble. We should be able to get to the postage office if we cut down here." He took her hand and they pushed through the crowds. There were a lot of people and someone bumped into her quite hard.

"My apologies," the person said. Cass glanced at him, ready to say it was all right, but she froze. It was the dark-haired man. They locked eyes and he smiled at her. Dacha pulled Cass away before she could reply.

They found the postage office and Cass sent her letters. But she couldn't stop thinking about the man and kept scanning the crowds. She must tell Captain Toskil when they got back.

"You seem distracted," Dacha said as they walked back to the inn.

"Sorry," Cass replied, forcing herself to be normal. "It's nothing. Tell me, I've been in the Islands for the last few months, is the Free Magic movement becoming more of a thing?"

"It does seem to be. And with all the rumours about Veraklia…"

"What rumours?" Cass asked.

Dacha glanced round to check that there was no

one listening to them. "That Queen Vegna has a magician working for her," he said.

"No!" Cass exclaimed. "But that's terrible. Why don't the enforcers stop her?"

Dacha shrugged. "I don't know, but you would have thought that Veraklia would have learned its lesson in the Magical Wars. I think that's the main reason for this trip – so Arden can discuss the situation with King Hoff."

"Really?" Cass said, digesting this information. It would certainly make sense of the meeting with Taryn. She thought briefly of Idaliz and wondered how she was getting on. "Did you grow up in Veraklia?" she asked Dacha.

"Until I was seven and then we moved to Minaris. My parents were goldsmiths and once the reserves ran out, so did their trade. They moved looking for work."

"And do you like Minaris?"

"I do," he replied. "But I miss Veraklia too. Until they shut the borders I used to spend every summer there with my grandfather. He had a farm up in the mountains and I loved going there. Sadly he died a few years ago."

"I'm so sorry," Cass said and they walked on. They reached the square where the inn was and were about to go back into it when a couple of girls came running up to Cass, singing,

"Oh, I'm the Queen of Minaris
And all the ladies have to curtsy to me,
Curtsy to me,
Curtsy to me,
In the City of the Fish."

And as they said fish they drew out *shhhh* just as the girl had in Aravura.

Cass felt a stab of alarm. It couldn't be a coincidence, surely? The girls turned to run but she grabbed one of them by the arm.

"Did someone tell you to sing that to me? A man with dark hair? Did he pay you?" she demanded but the girl laughed at her, repeated the shhhh and with a swift movement shook Cass off before she and her friend sprinted away. Cass let them go but her eyes darted around the square, searching for any sign of the man.

Dacha was bewildered. "Why are you so upset? They're children and it was just a nursery rhyme. Why would anyone pay them to sing it?" he asked her.

Cass opened her mouth to tell him and then realized she shouldn't – she needed to keep her role as Arden's sword as secret as she could, and besides, only Captain Toskil knew of her suspicions. So she replied, "Nothing," and Dacha, although he looked at her strangely, didn't ask her any further questions as they went back into the inn.

She went straight to see Captain Toskil who received the news with concern. "I will post extra men all around the queen's rooms and keep up a patrol in the square."

But the night passed peacefully and the day dawned bright and clear. Crossing the Forest of Thunt was a full day's journey so they set off when it was only just light, with plans to breakfast once they had covered some distance.

For as long as anyone had dwelt in the world, people had lived in the ancient Forest of Thunt. The trees provided shelter and firewood, and the woods were full of good food – venison, hare, mushrooms, lichen and berries. The

Thuntians still lived in tree houses and were mostly woodsmen, skilled in snake-catching, tree-climbing, mushroom-picking and the like. But once, hundreds of years ago, they were the most skilled magicians and apothecaries of their time, and people said that a certain type of magic still lingered there.

Despite the forest being home to the Sins, Arden was in a good mood, perhaps because, as she told Cass while she helped her dress, the forest was always pleased to see her. "My great-grandmother was Thuntian and my cousin Maer lives just the other side of it," she explained. "I used to come here every autumn for a couple of weeks – we had such a time of it, running wild in the forest. That was before the Sins of course. They've changed everything here," she added with a sigh.

"Why can't they be found?" Cass asked. "The forest isn't so large."

Arden shrugged. "I don't understand it either. I can only think that they move around constantly, and perhaps a share of their robbing goes to the Thuntians to pay for their silence. But they must be brought to justice. It is terrible for trade if nothing else, and so it's one of the things I am going to discuss with King Hoff. I am going to propose that we each provide soldiers to patrol the road to try and keep travellers safe."

Captain Toskil had decided that it was safer, in case of an attack, for Arden to be on horseback, so Cass pointed out that she should therefore ride too. Dacha found a sprightly-looking bay called Daisy for her and he held the horse while Cass got on. Cass could see that he was expecting she would be hopeless, but Cass was a naturally gifted rider and she sat easily on Daisy, holding the reins confidently.

Cass trotted off to join Arden, smiling to herself at the surprise on Dacha's face.

It was the perfect day to be riding, with a bright sun and deep blue sky, and the forest looked lovely, twinkling under its blanket of snow. They saw deer and elk, and hares darted across the road in front of them. Cass's eyes gobbled up the beauty of it all.

"Look! A woodland warbler!" Arden pointed as a bright blue bird flew just above their heads, singing a loud, throaty song. It hovered there for several minutes.

"It's back," Dacha remarked.

Arden looked at him with surprise.

"Cass and I saw one when we stopped in the woods before," Dacha explained.

"Well, even though I doubt it's the same one, I'm sure it's a good omen. Everyone knows how lucky they are," Arden said.

They stopped very briefly for breakfast in a tiny village that was really just a collection of tree houses perched high up in the sentian oaks, connected by a network of rope bridges. The Thuntians were delighted to see such important visitors and brought them hot venison pasties and red tea.

The party continued on their way and as the day passed, the woods grew gradually denser and the patches of bright blue sky above their heads seemed a long way away through the criss-cross of dark branches. Although the forest was still beautiful, Cass's feelings of unease began to trickle back. She felt as if they were being watched and whenever she turned her head she was sure she saw something move.

At midday, they stopped again for a picnic lunch and to rest the horses in a pretty glade. But delightful as it was to look at, Cass couldn't shake her apprehension. She felt sure that something was about to happen.

The most notorious spot for bandit attacks was a steep ravine known as the Choke, which they were to pass through not long after lunch. So as they left the glade Captain Toskil rearranged the order of the riders. He would ride first with Arden behind, flanked by two guards. Cass would follow next, with the others falling in behind the sledges. Cass could see everyone stiffen as they set off, braced for trouble.

The road dropped down sharply into the narrow valley and then twisted along several bends for half a mile or so before climbing sharply up again. They had been trotting up until now, but Captain Toskil cried, "I suggest we take this at a canter," and everyone quickened their pace. Cass looked nervously at the steeply sloped forest on either side of them, expecting to see a gang of robbers come careering down.

However, nothing happened. They passed through the ravine without seeing anyone else on the road and came up the other side. The forest opened out a little, and Cass felt she could breathe again. They all slowed their pace back to a trot and there was a collective sense of relief. There were only another eight miles or so until they reached the edge of the forest and Maer's castle was just beyond there.

Shortly after, they slowed down to cross a stone bridge over the river. Captain Toskil looked at the sky and announced, "We should hurry – the weather is closing in."

Cass was about to laugh at him, for the sky was bright blue with not a cloud in sight, but then Arden agreed. "I don't like the look of those clouds."

Cass hesitated before contradicting the queen, but she felt she had to speak out. "There are no clouds," she said tentatively. Everyone turned and stared at her. "There are no clouds at all – the sky is blue," she continued. "It's a conjuring trick. The forest, or someone, is up to mischief," she said, and then explained about being an obtuse.

It took everyone a moment to process what

she had said. "What do you want to do, Your Majesty?" Captain Toskil asked.

Arden looked around, her eyes flitting nervously. "I don't think we have any choice but to press on, as quickly as possible," she replied. "We can only be a few miles from Maer's house."

They rode on at a canter, but before they had covered more than a mile everyone began to slow their horses right down and squint into the road as if they couldn't see anything. Cass pulled her horse up next to Dacha.

"What's the matter?" she asked him.

"It seems as if we're in the middle of a snowstorm," Dacha said anxiously.

Cass was about to reply when an arrow whizzed past her ear.

"We're being attacked!" Captain Toskil shouted as several more arrows flew at them out of the sky. He was frantically looking around, blinded by the snow, but Cass, her heart pounding with adrenalin, could clearly see a number of men sitting up in the trees, drawn bows in their hands.

"It's a gang of men, about five of them, up in

the trees," she called to Captain Toskil, her voice quick with fear.

"Take the queen!" he ordered her. "We will hold them off. It is only another couple of miles to Maer's house. We'll meet you there."

Cass urged her horse over to Arden who had heard the conversation and looked as frightened as the others.

"Here, Your Majesty, give me your reins," Cass said to her, and when Arden handed them over, Cass kicked Daisy who responded immediately and both horses cantered off.

After about ten minutes of riding the horses as hard as they could, Cass dared to look behind them. With a sickening lurch in her stomach she saw that they were being followed by two men on horseback, handkerchiefs pulled up over their faces. They were some distance behind but when Cass looked again a few minutes later, she realized the men were swiftly gaining on them. She could not hope to defend Arden against both of them.

"Has the snow cleared for you?" she shouted to Arden.

"Just about," the queen responded.

"Good," Cass replied and slowed down enough to hand her back the reins. "We're being followed," she said and Arden looked behind.

"You need to gallop to Maer's house while I try to delay them," Cass said. She could see Arden about to object. "Please, Your Majesty," Cass said. "It's the only way. I cannot fight both of them for long." Arden gave a nod and then did as Cass said.

Cass wheeled Daisy round to face the men, placing herself diagonally across the road to try and stop them chasing Arden. As they drew near, despite the handkerchiefs covering their faces, Cass recognized one of them as the dark-haired man.

"So you want to fight?" he said mockingly as he pulled his horse up next to her. The other man hung slightly behind.

"I do," Cass replied as casually as she could.

"Very good. I think we'll take it in turns," the dark-haired man said to his friend. "Otherwise it seems a little unfair. I'll go first. Shall we dismount? I would so hate for the horses to get hurt."

Cass nodded curtly and swung herself down

from Daisy, feeling a flash of relief that they weren't going after Arden. But she didn't have a chance to consider this further because the dark-haired man slid off his horse, drew his sword and they began. *He fights like a bandit*, Cass thought after a few seconds. He fought with no finesse but a good deal of brute strength and intense determination, wielding his sword at her like a rolling pin. She deflected his parries and managed to nick his cheek, but then he lunged successfully at her and she lost her footing as he fenced her off the road and into the deep snow. Cass stumbled and he knocked her sword out of her hand. He grabbed her but then was distracted for a second by shouts from the road ahead.

"Maer's guards are coming!" the other man warned.

The dark-haired man swore and yanked Cass towards his horse as she saw the cavalcade of horses thundering towards them, with Arden and another woman at their head. *Yes!* Cass thought. She kicked him with all her might and tried to punch him in the face but he wouldn't let her go. He slung her over his horse face down like a sack of potatoes and jumped on, holding her arms tightly.

The horse swung round and Cass, who could see nothing, heard an arrow fly through the air above her.

"Arghh!" the man shouted as it hit him in the arm. The pain was just enough to make him loosen his grip on Cass and she flung herself backwards off the horse, landing heavily in the snow. Maer's men were upon them and the pair, knowing they would be defeated, wheeled their horses round and galloped off.

"Cass!" Arden cried, leaping down from her horse. "Are you all right?"

"Yes," Cass panted, still out of breath from the fight. She retrieved her sword and put it away.

"Shall we go after them, Your Majesty?" one of the riders asked Arden.

"Yes, please!" she replied. "And you should find the Queen's Guard and the rest of your men on the road too. They were attacked further back." She let out a sigh of concern. "I do hope they are OK."

A woman dressed in green velvet rode up to

them. "Cass, this is my friend the Countess Maer," Arden introduced her. "This is Cass, one of my ladies-in-waiting."

The woman said, arching an eyebrow, "I wish my lady's maid could fight like that – I would never feel unsafe again."

"Cass is a woman of many accomplishments," Arden replied. "Now, let's get to your house as quickly as possible, before some other disaster befalls us."

An hour later Cass was sitting by a crackling fire, drinking winter wine in the Great Hall of Castle Maer. The venerable knight himself was sitting opposite her and they were alone. Arden, along with the countess, was waiting anxiously in the hall for the arrival of the others.

"Tell me what happened, Cass," Maer said.

Cass explained about the attack in the snowstorm, and that being an obtuse meant she could see it was a conjuring trick.

"How many men were there?"

"About five," Cass replied. "Up in the trees."

Maer nodded. "That sounds like the Sins but I have never known them to use magic before, although strange things do often occur in the woods. I can only think that they were fortunate enough to be able to exploit the forest's mischief. Did you get a good look at any of the men?"

"Only the two men who attacked us later." She explained how she had taken Arden away from the ambush and that two men had come after them.

"What did they look like?"

Cass told him about the dark-haired man, and how she had seen him in Aravura and then again in Jena and Danske, and gave a sketchier version of his accomplice.

Maer had been nodding thoughtfully as she spoke and when she finished he said, "That sounds like a man named Wern – one of the ringleaders of the Sins."

"Isn't there one man who's the overall leader?" Cass asked.

Maer shook his head. "No, there doesn't appear to be. There are a few key men who run things. Wern is one and there's another couple named

Brun and Levi. There was a man called Zirt who looked like he would take charge about a year ago but he disappeared. These men often go off to work as mercenaries – they'll fight for anyone who pays them enough silvers."

Cass gave a start at the name Zirt. Perhaps it was a common name in Bunderland, but she couldn't help but say, "I came across a man named Zirt who joined the pirates in the Islands about six months ago. A tall blond northerner with bright blue eyes and a scar on his cheek."

"That sounds like him," Maer said. "How strange." He thought for a moment. "Or perhaps it's not. Perhaps he fell out with the Sins and decided to try his hand with some other thuggish thieves."

"Maybe," Cass agreed. But she felt that there was some connection she couldn't see yet, like a puzzle she didn't have all the pieces for.

"Anyway, you should be rid of them now. I have never heard of the Sins venturing further north than the forest."

The sound of people arriving in the hall brought both of them to their feet and they hurried out to find the rest of the party arriving. Cass couldn't see Dacha and she felt her stomach contract with fear.

"Everyone unharmed, Toskil?" Maer asked.

"A few minor injuries among my soldiers but nothing serious, thank goodness," Captain Toskil answered and Cass let herself relax. The captain went on, "The attackers withdrew pretty quickly after the queen left."

"Have your injured men brought into the kitchen – they can be treated there. Then please come with me, we can discuss matters further," Maer said to him.

Cass went over to Tiger who looked shaken but she smiled brightly at Cass. "You're a heroine! But you look all done in. Go and have a rest – I can manage this."

Cass accepted gratefully. The stress of the afternoon combined with the wine had made her feel exhausted. A maid showed her up to her little cubbyhole of a room off Arden's suite and she lay down on the bed. Although her eyes were heavy, she rubbed them fiercely as she wanted to stay awake for long enough to think everything through while it was fresh in her mind.

Cass was almost certain that the two men who had attacked them, Wern and his accomplice, were the same ones that had broken into the inn two nights before. They were clearly robbers, attracted presumably by the queen's jewels. But there were a couple of questions that remained for Cass about this. If they were after the queen's jewels then why had they not centred their attack on the luggage and the sledges? Captain Toskil said they had withdrawn almost as soon as she and Arden had left. Why had Wern not pursued Arden rather than staying and fighting Cass? Why was he paying children to scare her by singing nursery rhymes? Why bother? And how did Zirt fit into any of this, if he did at all?

She had no answers and Cass eventually drifted off to sleep, her brain still worrying.

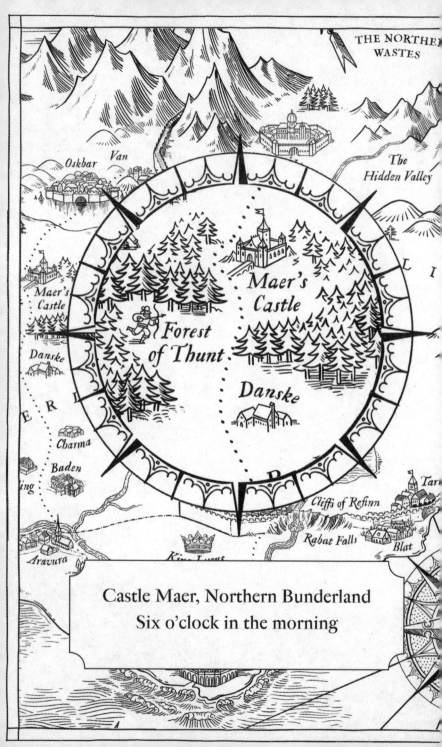

Castle Maer, Northern Bunderland
Six o'clock in the morning

7

The Ice Fair

They left at dawn the following day, accompanied by a large contingent of Maer's men. Arden was pale but cheerful, intensely relieved that they should reach Oskbar that night.

"And you know," she said to Cass and Tiger as they sat bundled up in the sledge, "I am tempted to sail back to Minaris via Pinoa. I would rather put up with winter storms than repeat the journey we have had."

The Forest of Thunt marked the transition between the fertile lowlands of Bunderland and the highlands that eventually became the mountain range of Suz. The road steadily climbed as the landscape folded itself into steep hills around them. Then at about noon the road swooped into the enormous Roer Valley, which ended after about twenty miles in the Lake of Glass. The City of Oskbar was on a large hilly island in the middle of the lake, and the road became busy with all the traffic journeying to and from the capital. Cass was still wary but with the extra guards and the amount of people around, an attack seemed unlikely so she allowed herself to relax a little and enjoy the scenery. It was still daylight when the sledges left the land and slid on to the broad causeway that led across the lake to Oskbar. Cass stuck her head out of the window to see the city ahead of them, rising like an iron fist out of the frozen lake.

The ancient City of Oskbar was divided into five areas, one for each of the great knighting families. Brightly coloured banners lined the streets, marking their territories and flapping in the wind like birds' wings, and bitter rivalries existed between them. But two parts of the city remained neutral – the palace, which was at its very centre, and the famous Ice Fair, that in the winter months spilled out over the frozen lake like a flaming petticoat. It was protected from ice wolves by high wooden fences and at night it was lit up by hundreds of torches, lamps and candles. Cass thought how amazing it looked as they passed by, riding up to the city gates.

Arden was popular in Oskbar, so there was much cheering from people on the streets as they wound their way up to the palace. Cass looked out of the sledge window and formed a vague impression of tall grey-stone buildings with deep roofs like hats above them, divided by narrow flights of stairs. It was much too steep for skating and the snow had been cleared from the pavements and stairs to allow people to walk. But Cass noticed that by the side of the road and the stairs were broad sunken channels, which were still coated with a thick layer of ice.

"What are those for?" she asked Tiger.

"Sledshots," she replied. But before Cass could ask any more, Tiger announced, "Oh, look, we are arriving," and started to fuss about Arden's coat and hair.

The palace reminded Cass of one of those dolls

that split down the middle to reveal another doll, and then another, and then yet another. It was a fortress, within a fortress, and then as they were ushered through another set of gates, guarded by armoured knights, they came to the Tower of Usk. This stood at the very centre of the palace and it was where King Hoff and his family lived and Arden was to stay. Cass felt a rush of relief looking at its sheer walls and the armies of guards swarming around. How could Arden not be safe here?

The following morning, Tiger woke Cass with a gentle shake and a cup of bitter tea. "Sorry, have I overslept?" Cass apologized, seeing the daylight seeping in around the curtains. It had been late by the time Arden had come to bed.

Tiger smiled. "Not really. Arden is still asleep too but I need to wake her soon, so you'd better get dressed now. King Hoff is expecting her in an hour. Oh, by the way, these were brought up for you." She handed her some letters. Cass recognized Mrs Pott's, Tig's and Rip's writing with a smile.

"You'd better read them later," Tiger added.

The hour passed quickly in a whirl of bathing, breakfast, dressing, the breathing-in and lacing, the fluffing and arranging, until Arden, looking serene, floated off to talk politics with King Hoff. Cass questioned whether she should accompany her but Arden had laughed, saying, "I am quite safe here. Besides the Bundish would think it most peculiar."

So Cass helped Tiger clear up and finish the unpacking. By the middle of the morning, Tiger announced that all was done and Cass was free to do as she pleased for the rest of the day. With a stab of delight she returned to her bedroom, lay down on her extremely comfortable bed and tore open the letter from Rip first.

Dear Cass, it began. *I can't believe you will be reading this in Oskbar – is it snowing?*

Yes, it is, Cass thought, looking out of the window, *but only a bit.* She was about to read on when she was interrupted by a knock at her door. "Come in!" she called, putting her letter down and getting off her bed. She expected it to be Tiger but to her surprise it was Dacha.

"Hello," he said, coming into the room. He was wearing normal clothes, which made him look different. Older somehow and smaller.

"Hello," Cass replied. "Does Captain Toskil want to see me?"

"No," Dacha replied, looking slightly embarrassed. "I have the rest of the day off and Tiger told me that you do too, so I wondered if you would like to come to the Ice Fair with me." Then regaining a little bit of his cockiness he added, "It can be a little rough and I thought you might need my protection." Dacha had been teasing her about being the queen's sword ever since the Forest of Thunt.

"How kind of you," Cass replied, rolling her eyes. "But yes, I'd love to come to the fair. Also, can you explain what a sledshot is?"

"I can indeed. In fact, I'll show you what a sledshot is."

Cass changed out of her lady-in-waiting clothes then followed Dacha down through the tower to the cellars and kitchens in the basement.

"Sledshot?" he asked a servant, who cocked his head in a direction in reply.

"Ahh, here we go," Dacha announced, leading Cass out into a small courtyard with a tunnel at one end of it. It was about as high as a man and just a little broader, and running into it were two channels. Next to it was a row of large high-sided sledges. Two boys were turning a wheel, bringing the sledges back up full of food and drink, while several others were unloading the contents on to trolleys.

"Those are sledshots," Dacha said, gesturing with a flourish to the sledges. "It's how they transport everything around the city," he explained. "And it's how the Oskbarians get where they want to go in a hurry."

"How clever," Cass replied.

"Right, let's have a go then," Dacha said.

"Really?" Cass asked hesitantly, feeling a pang of misgiving as she looked into the dark tunnel.

Dacha burst out laughing. "So you're quite happy to fight off robbers but you're scared of a sledshot?"

Cass smiled in response but said, "Are you sure it's not dangerous?"

"Only if you try to stop it," he replied. "You have

103

to just trust in the sledshot. I'd better sit in front so I can steer, in case you find it too alarming. They do go pretty fast."

Cass was still looking warily at the sledges and the tunnel when an elderly lady appeared, grandly dressed like a courtier. One of the boys immediately came and helped her into a sledge and she shot off down the tunnel.

Dacha arched an eyebrow at Cass. "Still scared?"

Cass laughed. "I'm sure you arranged that on purpose. I am still a bit frightened but let's try it," she replied and they got into a sledge.

This is amazing! Cass thought as they flew off at great speed, but then they slammed into a small metal gate that had shut across their path as another sledge whizzed past in front of them.

They set off again and Dacha steered them off to the right, following a sign for the Ice Fair. It was a steep, straight run down with no other routes crossing it so they picked up speed quickly. Cass felt as if they were flying as the sledge raced along, weaving between the buildings, making her heart pound. Seconds later, they were catapulted through an arch in the city walls and came to a standstill at the sledshot station at the Ice Fair.

"Fun?" Dacha asked.

"Really good fun," Cass replied with a laugh, getting out of the sledge. "Can we do it again?"

"Well, the slight problem is you have to walk all the way back up to the palace; people don't get hauled up. Anyway, there's a lot more fun to be had here," he said, looking out at the fair. Cass followed his eyes and a sea of colour hit her – the maze of brightly coloured stalls, the mechanical fairground rides and the entertainment tents. She inhaled the smell of spiced cakes and winter wine and felt a thrill of delicious excitement.

"Is there anything you particularly want to do or shall we just wander around?" Dacha asked.

"I want to see everything," Cass announced. But then something caught her eye in the distance – an enormous grey creature waving a nose like a snake. She gasped and shrieked in excitement. "An elephant!! I have wanted to see one for my whole life. My father used to tell me stories about them when I was tiny. Please can we go and see that first!"

Dacha laughed. "Of course we can. The animal

circus is one of the best bits."

They must have spent at least an hour watching the animals and then with no further plan, they meandered along, stopping to see whatever they fancied and play whichever games caught their eye. Cass felt herself finally relax and shed her layers of worry.

At noon they ate hot spicy sausages and watched a troupe of acrobats.

"That used to be me," Cass told Dacha and when he looked puzzled she explained. "I used to be an acrobat on the Circus Boat."

"Really? You are full of surprises. Why did you give it up?"

"It gave me up," Cass replied. "I broke my wrist badly and that was that."

"Don't you miss it?" Dacha asked.

Cass considered his question.

"Yes, I do. It was always my dream since I was a little child and letting go of your dreams is never easy."

Dacha nodded seriously.

"And what's your dream now?"

Cass thought about the Company of Eight, but

since they were a secret organization she couldn't very well mention them to Dacha. So she replied, "A mooncake."

Dacha burst out laughing.

"Let me make your dream come true," he said extravagantly, and bought them a couple of the blisteringly hot cakes and cups of sweet winter wine. They watched a mechanical puppet show – a comic version of the old story of Nirzad and the swans – which made them both giggle and then went into a hall of mirrors.

Still laughing, they walked on. "This must be the magical district," Dacha said, looking at all the signs for fortune tellers and trancers.

Sure enough, a child came dancing up to them. "You must come and see my mother. She is the best trancer and fortune teller in the whole of the Longest World." The girl looked Veraklian, with long copper hair and fair freckly skin.

"Really?" Dacha asked, playing along.

"Absolutely," the child replied. "Tonight she will have a queue of a thousand people waiting for a reading but now, by your incredible good luck, she is free."

"Goodness me, that is fortunate," Dacha replied earnestly.

"It is a miracle," the child replied. "She is very reasonable, only two silvers for a reading, so you must come."

"I'm an obtuse so don't ask me," Cass said. The girl looked at her in amazement but seeing there were no silvers to be made out of Cass, she quickly turned her attention to Dacha.

He was clearly reluctant so she changed her approach. "Please come," she pleaded. "We haven't eaten yet today or last night. You won't regret it, she's honestly amazing."

"Why don't you?" Cass said, feeling sorry for the child.

Dacha considered it. "She's a good trancer, you say?"

The child nodded vigorously.

"Very well then," he said. "Take us to her."

It was one of the smaller, shabbier tents and it was chilly inside with the brazier only giving off the most meagre heat. The young woman who came forwards had a bright smile but Cass thought how tired and underfed she looked.

"Please come in," she said. "Is it both of you?" she asked but before they could answer, she looked at Cass and said, "Oh, but no, you are an obtuse. How extraordinary. Come, sit down." She led them to a pile of floor cushions around the brazier.

"Zena, fetch some tea," she said to the girl. "So, how can I help you?" she asked Dacha as Zena handed around the tiny beakers of steaming tea.

"I have some family in Veraklia – an uncle and an aunt. I wanted to see how they were," Dacha said.

The woman's smile faltered. "I will try to trance them," she said. "But it has proved very difficult in Veraklia. It is almost as if someone has put up an invisible wall around the country so our minds cannot enter it. All the trancers are saying the same thing, I promise you."

"Never mind," said Dacha breezily. "Will you tell me how my parents are? They are in Minaris."

"Of course," she said, relieved. "Here, give me your hands and picture them and where they live in Minaris for me. It will take me a few minutes."

She took Dacha's hands and they both shut their eyes. Cass drank her tea and looked around the tent at the bedding rolls and the battered trunk of clothes. *How cold it must be at night*, she thought.

"I can see them," the woman announced. "Your father is sitting at a desk, writing. Perhaps he is a scribe?"

"He is a sum keeper," Dacha replied, sounding impressed.

"Your mother has just brought him his lunch and now she is with someone else, a young woman and two young children."

"That'll be my sister," Dacha said.

"They all look well and happy," the woman said with a smile, dropping his hands and opening her eyes.

Dacha thanked her and gave her two silvers. They all got up and then something very strange happened. The woman gave a slight cry and doubled over as if in pain. Dacha and Cass turned to help her but Zena rushed forwards and pulled her back on to the cushions.

"This happens sometimes. She's very sensitive," she explained.

The woman had her eyes closed but then opened them suddenly, saying to Dacha in a whisper,

"Be careful, you must be very careful. At the world's end, you are in great danger." And she slumped back, her eyes shut.

"Will she be all right?" Dacha asked.

"Yes, yes, she'll be fine," Zena said, practically shooing them out of the tent.

"Well, that was odd," Dacha said lightly to Cass once they were out of earshot. "You would have thought we would all be in great danger at the world's end."

Cass smiled, relieved that he wasn't upset by the fortune teller's words. "But perhaps because you're so special, you will be the only one to survive."

Dacha laughed. "I'm so pleased that at long last you've realized how special I am. Now, I'm hungry again," Dacha said. "Come on, I'll buy you a venison pie."

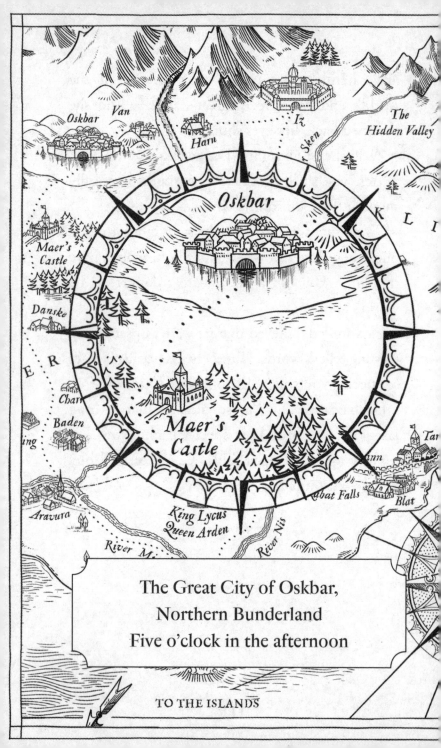

The Great City of Oskbar,
Northern Bunderland
Five o'clock in the afternoon

TO THE ISLANDS

8

Hush, Cassandra

The sun was setting as they walked back up the steep, twisting cobbled streets to the palace, stopping to look at some of the stalls that lined the way. It was traditional to give small presents at the Mid-Winter Feast so Cass bought a few things for Mrs Potts, Lin and Tig, as did Dacha for his family.

"My brother will be racing," Dacha said as they discussed the Feast.

"In the Ice Race on the River Mira? Really?" Cass asked. "Is he fast? Does he stand a chance of winning?"

Dacha laughed. "He's not slow but I don't think

he'll win. He'd have to beat Minin – he's won for the last few years."

"Oh, I missed it last year. I was on the Island of Women." Cass was about to go on when a young boy tapped her on the shoulder.

Cass turned around and he said, "Excuse me, miss, but I've got a message for you," and he began to sing,

"Oh, I'm the Queen of Minaris
And all the ladies have to curtsy to me,
Curtsy to me,
Curtsy to me,
In the City of the Fish."

And, just as the girls had in Aravura and Danske, as he said fish he drew out *shhhh*.

Cass felt the blood drain from her face. Wern must have followed them. The boy turned to sprint away but Cass grabbed his arm.

"Who told you to sing that to me? Who sent you?" she demanded.

"I don't know who she was. A lady, just a lady," the boy said, struggling to get away.

Cass had been expecting him to give a description of Wern. She faltered. "A lady?" she queried.

"Yes," the boy replied.

"What did she look like?"

"Very beautiful. Dressed like a courtier."

Who in the Longest World could that be? Cass thought. "Where was she?"

"Just in the street, over there," he said, gesturing. "But she's gone now," he added unnecessarily.

Cass let the boy go as there didn't seem much point in doing anything else. But she felt shot through with anxiety. It must be a warning about the queen. Arden was in danger.

"I must get back to the palace," she said to Dacha.

"Of course, but can you explain? What does the rhyme mean?"

Cass explained to him briefly about the girl in Aravura and Wern as they marched back.

"I understand why you are concerned, but really the queen will be quite safe in the palace."

"She is due to go out tonight to a reception in the city, isn't she?" Cass asked.

"You're right," Dacha replied, his confidence faltering. "At a noble's house. Perhaps we should tell Captain Toskil to send more men."

"Yes, definitely, and I must go with her as well as Tiger," Cass said as they reached the palace.

The first thing Cass did was try to find Captain Toskil. But he was out on a tour of the fortifications so she had to just leave a note for him. Then she went back to the queen's rooms where she found Tiger lying on her bed, looking very pale.

"Cass, I'm sorry, it must have been something I ate. My stomach is terrible so you will have to accompany the queen to the dinner this evening." Cass could hear in her voice how ill she felt.

"Of course, that's fine," Cass replied. "Where exactly is it?" she asked.

"It's at one of the mansions just below the palace. You'll need to wear your silk evening dress so why don't you go and get ready while Arden is still in talks. You know what a rush it will be once she's back, and the sledges are due at six thirty. I've laid out her dress on her bed and she is to wear the diamond-and-sapphire tiara."

Cass nodded and said, "You should sleep now. Is there anything I can get you?"

"No, thank you," Tiger said, shutting her eyes.

Rip's letter was still lying on Cass's bed, so she quickly put on her gilded dress, neatened up her hair and then, after stowing her knife in her pocket, she sat down to read it. It was mostly chat about what he had been doing but there was a paragraph at the end that made her pause.

By the way, I don't know if word has reached you from another source but the pirate Zirt has managed the almost impossible and escaped from Prison Island. He must have had help from outside.

Cass felt a jolt of shock. Zirt had escaped... What could that mean? She began to think it through but she was distracted by Arden's return. The queen looked fed up.

"Tea, please, Cass. I need to write a note to Lycus to go by bird and then I had better get ready for this wretched dinner. Where's Tiger?"

"She's ill, I'm afraid. So I'll come with you tonight instead, if you're happy with that?"

"Of course. Poor Tiger. I will go and check on

her in a minute. Now I understand why you're all dressed up," Arden replied. Then with a smile that warmed her face a little she said, "It'll be nice, you can laugh with me at all the pompous Oskbarians."

Cass scooted around getting tea and Arden insisted that Cass take the message for Lycus to the birdhouse herself to ensure that no one read it. Cass tried to find Captain Toskil again but he was still out. By the time she got back it was time for Arden's bath and dressing. There wasn't another moment to try to see him before six thirty came and they had to leave for the evening.

They were to travel to the party with King Hoff and the rest of the royal family in a fleet of their sledges. Dacha and three other guards were waiting for them at the palace entrance. *Four guards should be enough*, Cass thought nervously.

The mansion was only a short sledge ride away. The house itself was set back behind a courtyard garden, like the grand houses in the Islands, and protected from the street by high walls. The courtyard was lit up with torches and every window in the house was filled with candles and oil lamps. It had started to snow again; big fat flakes that drifted gently down from the sky.

It was the first large public engagement that Cass had been to with Arden and she wasn't quite prepared for all the fuss. The party was being held in a grand room at the back of the house and their route to the room was lined with people who bowed and curtsied to King Hoff and Arden. Once they entered the room, the king took Arden's hand, saying, "Ladies and gentlemen, please join me in welcoming our dear friend Arden, formerly princess of our great allies Pinoa and now Queen Arden of Minaris."

There was cheering and everyone rushed forwards to speak to Arden. Cass stood at her side and slightly behind – not near enough to hear conversations properly but close enough if Arden needed anything. Servants were circulating, carrying large silver platters of food and goblets of winter wine. Arden reached for one. Musicians played as they walked between the groups and jugglers and tricksters kept everyone entertained.

Arden greeted many people, but after a while they fell back and she became absorbed in an intense conversation with an elderly gentleman who she appeared to know very well. They spoke in low voices so Cass couldn't hear what they were saying.

Arden had finished her winter wine and turned briefly to Cass, to hand her the glass. "Could you get me another, please, Cass?"

"Of course," Cass replied but at that moment a serving girl appeared with four glasses arranged on her tray. She picked one off and handed it to the queen. It wasn't customary for a servant to hand glasses to a queen and Cass was about to object. But Arden took it and began to drink, so Cass stepped back.

It was about ten minutes later that Cass noticed Arden swaying a little and her hand reaching up to her head. "Cass, could you fetch me a glass of water?" she said. Cass went straight to the kitchen, returning a few moments later.

"Thank you," Arden replied, taking the cold glass immediately and drinking from it.

She's very pale, Cass thought with concern. *I hope she isn't ill like Tiger.*

"You don't look well, Your Majesty. Come, let us sit down," the elderly courtier said as he led her over to some seats.

Arden sat down gratefully. "My apologies. My other lady-in-waiting is unwell and I rather fear that I have caught her illness. I think I'll return home. Let me just go and tell King Hoff, and Cass, will you arrange for a sledge?"

Cass nodded and rushed out of the room. She found Dacha hovering with the other guards.

"The queen is ill," she told them. "Can one of you fetch a sledge?"

"Of course," Dacha said, sounding concerned. "Can she walk? Does she need help?"

"You might want to come and take her arm and perhaps we should send for a doctor?" Cass was about to turn and go back in but Arden appeared on the arm of the elderly gentleman.

"Ah, Dacha," she said. "Will you come with me to the sledge? And Cass, please could you try and find where they've put my furs?"

The servant girl in charge of furs was young and confused, so it took her a little while to find Arden's cloak.

Cass looked for Arden in the hall. "She's already gone, miss," one of the servants told her. Cass looked out through the front door and saw her ahead with Dacha, clutching her stomach.

Oh dear! Cass thought. She pulled on her own fur hurriedly and rushed across the courtyard to join them, wrapping the fur around Arden's shoulders. It was still snowing a little.

"Just in time," Dacha said with a smile. "Here's the sledge." Cass followed his glance and assumed he was joking. It was a scruffy-looking closed sledge, driven by a couple of men with scarves pulled up over their faces against the cold.

But when it stopped and Dacha made as if to help Arden into it, Cass said, "Dacha, what are you doing? This isn't a royal sledge."

They both looked at her as if she were mad. "No, stop!" Cass cried. "It's another enchantment!"

As she said it, a woman's mocking voice spoke from the dark inside the sledge. "Hush, Cassandra! They can't hear you," and to Cass's amazement, the world stopped. Literally.

Arden and Dacha froze like statues in their positions, the snowflakes were suspended in mid-air. It was proper magic – not just illusion – but real, powerful magic and Cass needed a moment to take it in. Nothing, absolutely nothing, moved. There was no sound at all except for a thud as the men jumped down. One was Wern, and despite the scarf Cass knew instantly that the other was Zirt.

"No!" she cried, leaping in front of Arden. "You shall not take her."

Zirt laughed at her. "You just don't get it, kitten, do you? It's not the queen we want, it's you!"

And Cass was so surprised that she almost didn't resist as he grabbed her arms like she was a doll. He swiftly gagged her then trussed her up with ropes, shoving her into the back of the sledge, before they slid away into the night.

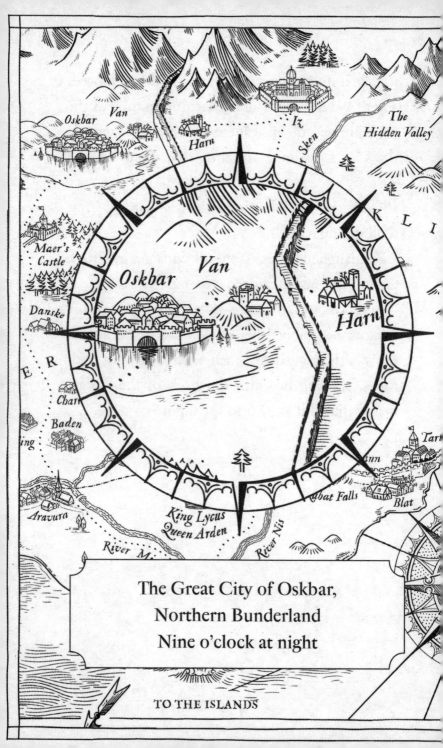

The Great City of Oskbar,
Northern Bunderland
Nine o'clock at night

TO THE ISLANDS

9

The Border Crossing

Outraged and seething with fury, Cass would have screamed at the woman who sat opposite her in the closed sledge if she hadn't had a gag in her mouth. For despite the gloom in the coach, despite the fact that she was so altered from the girl who Cass had known four years before in the Square of Seas, she instantly recognized the woman. It was Lin's sister, Nym. Her face, which had once been slightly plump, was now angular and her long black hair that had always just hung down her back was now piled up in an elaborate style. Her simple clothes had been replaced by a fur coat and jewels to rival Arden's. But her eyes remained the same – as cold and curious as a cat's.

Cass remembered her conversation with Lin about Nym before she left Minaris. Well, Nym most certainly wasn't in the Farthest Lands. She was causing trouble much closer to home. *But what in the world could Nym want with me?* Cass wondered furiously. *Why would she have bothered to hire the Sins to capture me? And how could I not have realized that Zirt and Wern were chasing me all along?* Cass berated herself. She remembered Zirt in the Islands always picking her to fight with, and then in the forest Wern had let Arden go. It was her they wanted. But why?

"Little Cassandra, all grown up," Nym said in a mocking tone, as if they were old friends who had unexpectedly bumped into each other. "I have you at last. You've led us a merry dance, first across the Islands and now up here. It's been quite the business – Zirt having to join the pirates to lure you to him, and then chasing you with that fool Arden. You've earned him a good deal of gold. By the way, did you like my snowstorm in the forest? And I hope you didn't mind me teasing you a little on the journey," and she began to sing in a childish voice. "Oh, I'm the Queen of Minaris…"

She stopped and laughed. "Of course, we had to make you think that it was the queen we were after, we didn't want you getting too suspicious. Now, let's see what you have in your pockets." She came over, sat next to Cass and frisked her pockets, pulling out her knife.

"I think I'd better take that," she remarked. Nym took Cass's hands and pulled off Lin's ring. She paused, considering it for a moment. "A present from my dear sister, I see," she said. "Well, I don't want her to be able to track you." She threw it out of the window. Then she grabbed Cass's citizen necklace – her Minarian fish – from around her neck. "This had better go too."

The sledge careered down the slippery lanes of the frozen city and only stopped when the way ahead of them was blocked at the city gates. Nym paused in her scrutiny of Cass and bowed her head, shutting her eyes just for a moment as if in prayer. The world froze again and their sledge made its way around the other sledges and out of the gates without any difficulty. Once they were on the causeway, Cass watched as out of the window the world came back to life. Where would they be headed? Back to the Forest of Thunt perhaps? Or to the port at Pinoa?

"If you are expecting to be rescued, you'll have a long wait," Nym said, as if she could read her mind. "The sledge is still enchanted, I'm afraid, so no one will see you in here. And back at the mansion, everyone's memory of what occurred is very hazy – did you go to fetch a doctor? Or have you made your own way to the palace? Besides, they are all quite properly much more worried over poor Arden," Nym said with pretend concern. "You," she added spitefully, "are only a lady-in-waiting, Cass. No one is going to send an army to look for you."

Cass knew that Nym was right. However she put the words out of her head and instead focused on testing the ropes that were binding her wrists and ankles. But they were tight and solid. Cass swore like a Minarian docker in her head.

After a while, Nym grew tired of inspecting Cass and closed her eyes. Cass was unsure if she actually slept, but she knew that there was little chance of sleeping herself she was so wound up. She gazed out at the inky night-time landscape and tried to calmly and logically work out why Nym would want to capture her. For her fighting skills? But that made no sense – there were plenty of skilled fighters in the world, why pick her? Was it something to do with the Company, or to do with Lin?

Eventually, exhausted by the thoughts bumping around her mind, Cass fell into a half sleep, only to be woken by the sledge stopping. The sky was lightening and Nym was gone. Cass looked out of the window. They appeared to be in a farmyard, but where it was, she had no idea. She struggled briefly with the knotted rope around her wrists to no avail, and then she saw Nym striding back towards the carriage, looking entirely out of place in the muddy yard in her ostentatious furs.

She carried a cup of water in her hand, which she put on the floor while she loosened Cass's gag. She then held the cup to her lips and let Cass drink.

When she had finished, Cass spluttered, "Why have you done this? What do you want with me? Where are we going?"

"I thought you would be full of annoying questions. You were always a most tiresome child," Nym said with a sigh. "I'm sorry but I can't be bothered to answer them now."

She put the gag back over Cass's mouth, ignoring her protests. "There, that's better," Nym announced. "All you need to know is that we'll be off again in a moment once they've changed the horses. Then we will reach the border by nightfall."

Which border? Cass speculated desperately. *The Minarian one? No, that would be too far away. The Pinoan one was much more likely and then on to a ship.* That would chime with Lin's theory that her sister was involved with the Magical Uprising in the Farthest Lands.

But then as Cass looked out of the window, she began to doubt her hunch. They seemed to be heading up into the mountains, and there weren't any mountains between Pinoa and Bunderland. Cass tried to remember her geography. The only mountains were to the north and east of Bunderland leading either to the Northern Wastes or to Veraklia. Both of these could be possible but why? Why would Nym be living in either of these places? Then Cass remembered with a sharp jolt something Dacha had said, when they were out together in Danske – that the Veraklian queen,

Vegna, was using a magician. Could that be where Nym had been? At the Veraklian court?

Cass didn't have to wait long to have her hunch confirmed. They passed a milestone in the road, which said, 'Veraklia seventy miles'. *Well, I suppose at least I know now*, Cass thought to herself, trying to dampen down some of the furious frustration that she felt. And perhaps, she thought, her spirits lifting slightly, Idaliz might still be there.

By the position of the sun, which shone for most of the day, Cass judged that they were heading fairly consistently east. They had kept to the main road and had passed through several villages and one large town, which Cass guessed was Van. Although the buildings and people looked unmistakably Bundish, the landscape changed as they came into the mountains proper. The broad valleys were shrinking and sharpening and the road was steadily climbing. The trees were changing to what Cass guessed were pinelets, which she had only seen before in pictures, and she caught glimpses of the mountain peaks beyond.

So if we were to cross the border tonight, Cass thought, picturing the map on the wall of her old classroom at Mrs Papworth's Academy, *where would we then be headed? Presumably to the capital, Iz?* Cass recalled it was known as the City of the Birds as it was so high up in the mountains. From memory Cass figured it would only be a day's ride or so from the border.

But before that they had to cross the border. How would Nym manage that? Would she freeze time again? The answer came soon enough, and when it did, it was nothing that she ever could have imagined.

Suddenly they veered off the main road, and rode along a track until they reached the yard of a derelict house, protected from views of the road by a line of conifers. Nym slunk out of the sledge and had a discussion with the men, just out of Cass's earshot. The horses were unbridled from the sledge and saddled up. Then Zirt undid the ropes around Cass's ankles and grabbed her by the arm.

"You're coming with me," he said, pulling her out of the sledge and shoving her up on to a large bay horse. He got up behind her and put one arm tightly around her waist, making Cass's skin crawl. She tried to focus on the others to distract herself.

Nym was already on horseback, looking confident but wary, glancing around her in the woods as if she was half expecting an attack. Wern had his back to Cass, fiddling with his saddle and adjusting the stirrups, before he mounted his horse. Once he was on they set off, taking a steep path that wound up through the pine forests until their way was blocked by a blank stretch of the Invincible Wall.

Cass had never seen the wall before and had to admit that it was incredibly impressive. It was made of bricks and was about fifteen metres high with a castellated top. She knew from her lessons that it was thick enough for five men to walk along it side by side and that it was often patrolled.

But I wonder why we've come here? Cass thought, looking at the blank expanse of bricks. She had expected to be taken to a fort or a gate with some means of crossing.

They stopped a little way back from the wall and Cass watched curiously as Nym nudged her horse nearer. Then she too halted, a couple of metres away. There was a sense of anticipation from the others and Cass felt herself sit up a little higher to see what Nym would do.

It started with a loud scraping noise. *What's that?* Cass looked around. And then she saw that hundreds of bricks that made up the section of wall in front of them were beginning to loosen. Cass watched, her eyes wide with wonder, as the bricks flew out of the wall one by one and bobbed, suspended in the air like a swarm of angry bees until there was a gap wide enough for them to ride through.

Nym gave a self-satisfied glance back at them. "Shall we go?"

Cass kept her face as blank as she could, determined not to show Nym how amazed she was.

"I'd better repair the damage or the queen will be furious with me," Nym said with a smirk when they had ridden through. She clicked her fingers and the bricks all flew back in place, as if they had never been moved. The men laughed sycophantically and Cass thought, *She may be paying them but they're still in awe of her.*

They followed a path back to the road, riding hard for the rest of the day and only stopping a couple of times briefly to change horses at shabby inns. At every point, Cass was alert to any means of escape, but there was never a moment when Zirt, Wern or Nym took their eyes off her. She also knew that even if she were to get away from them, staying hidden would be very difficult. Not only was she still wearing her lavish lady-in-waiting furs, she also had a look that came from having enough to eat and a relatively comfortable life, which set her apart from the rest of the population. And although the sight of a gagged girl attracted people's eyes, they looked away immediately, as they had obviously learned to do.

Only a couple of metres of wall may have separated Veraklia and Bunderland, but Cass felt as if she had entered a different world. Gone were the tidy Bundish farms, with cosy cottages and herds of quacking geese charging around pretty farmyards. Instead everywhere Cass looked was either ruined or hopelessly neglected.

Cass had imagined Veraklia would be like the red district, the area of Minaris where most of the Veraklian immigrants lived. It was one of Cass's favourite places – always brimming with life and colour. The buildings were painted with murals in vibrant pinks, greens and blues and the women dressed in similarly garish colours, their hair bound up in headscarves. There were food stalls on every street selling bowls of steaming, spicy noodles and toffee cakes, and multi-coloured kites flew from the rooftops, for the Veraklians all had what they called "skylust" – an obsession with everything to do with the sky. But the Veraklia that Cass found herself in was entirely different.

Some of the old farmhouses had the faded ghosts of the beautiful paintings that used to cover them and you could see the remnants of their green-tiled roofs, but these had mostly been replaced by a motley collection of old bits of timber. There were few animals around and those that Cass could see looked painfully thin. The Veraklians themselves looked little better – shivering in the bitter cold in old patched clothes, their faces pinched and haggard. Cass saw children with their feet bound in rags instead of shoes, working like adults. The poverty felt hopeless and oppressive.

When they passed through a couple of towns, she was shocked by the open sewers and piles of rubbish. The buildings were plastered in posters with slogans like 'Death to the Bundish!',

'Watch Your Neighbours!' and 'Foreign Spies are Everywhere!'. The last one made Cass shudder. *Let Idaliz be safe*, she prayed.

Cass also couldn't fail to notice all the soldiers. Almost every young man and woman, some no more than children, was dressed in the dark grey padded army coats, swords swinging by their sides.

In the late afternoon the road began to twist steeply up and the air became clearer and thinner. Cass could feel her breath quicken. As the daylight ebbed away, she could see the crags and peaks of the mountains rising above them. They must be nearing Iz.

The City of Iz lay in a bowl, cradled by mountain peaks on all sides. Its city walls rose up like sinister grey cliffs ahead of them. It was nearly dark as they approached and the city gates were shut for the night. But at the sight of Nym they swung open and the riders cantered in, barely breaking the horses' stride.

Inside the city the watchmen were lighting the coloured lanterns the city was famous for. But apart from them, the marble pavements were largely empty. There were none of the bustling night markets or overflowing inns that you would see in any other city in the Longest World in the evening.

The Winter Palace lay right at the top of the city, its back to the mountains. It only took a few minutes to canter through the empty streets. A stream of servants greeted their arrival and if Cass had ever doubted Nym's influence, these thoughts were banished by the bowing and scraping.

"Where do you want her?" Zirt asked Nym, referring to Cass as if she were a trunk. "The prison quarters like the enforcers?"

So that's why Nym hadn't been stopped, Cass grasped.

"No, I think the Slit is better for her," Nym replied.

Zirt took her to a narrow slither of a room with a door at one end and a barred window at the other. He undid the ropes around her wrists and ungagged her.

Cass immediately cried, "What am I doing here? Why have you taken me? Why won't you tell me?"

But he ignored her and slammed the thick timber door behind him. She heard him not only lock it with a key but pull across several bolts.

Brushing away tears of frustration, Cass looked around her. She had to admit that although it was hardly luxurious, it wasn't a dungeon either. There was glass in the window and a mattress on the floor with some bedding. A full pitcher of water, a washing bowl and a chamber pot were beside it. To Cass's surprise and relief there were a couple of candles and a bundle of firewood in the tiny fireplace and a box of matches.

As soon as Zirt had gone, Cass lit a candle and set about making a fire, which was soothing in itself, and soon orange flames were flickering over the wood. She sat down on the floor in front of it and tried to bring a bit of warmth back into her brain and body. Then, without warning, a hatch at the bottom of the door flew open and a tray was shoved through with a small loaf of bread and a bowl of stew on it. Cass, who was starving, fell on the food, wolfing it down in seconds. Feeling slightly more human, but more tired than ever, she got on to the mattress and wrapped herself up in the thin blankets. *Why am I here?* she wondered for the umpteenth time, before she fell into a long and dreamless sleep.

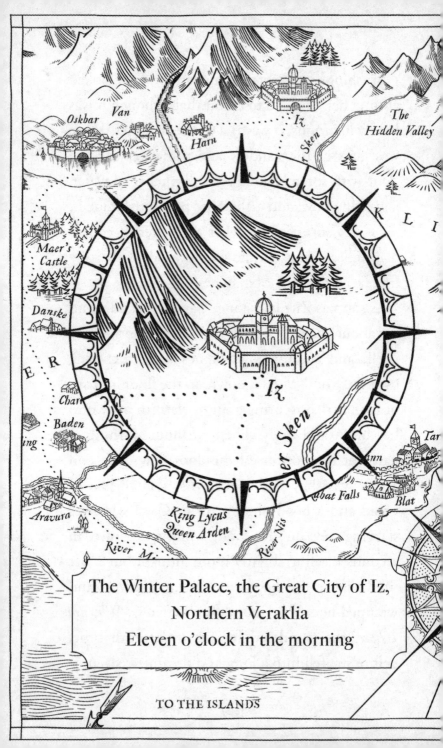

The Winter Palace, the Great City of Iz,
Northern Veraklia
Eleven o'clock in the morning

TO THE ISLANDS

Silence and Patience

Three guards accompanied Cass along the panelled corridors and narrow staircases of the Winter Palace as they took her to see Nym. One walked ahead while the other two took an arm each, one holding a knife to her ribs. If the servants they met in the corridors were surprised they hid it well.

It was clearly not the moment to try and escape, so Cass used her eyes well, studying the guards, working out how many weapons they had and considering how well trained they were likely to be. She looked all around her at the palace, not to admire the beautiful paintings of flowers and animals that covered the walls, but trying to glean as much about its layout as possible.

Nym's chambers were high up in a tower near the building's centre. The guards showed Cass into an octagonal room that resembled a library, lined with shelves of books and a high-domed ceiling. They left her, shutting the door behind them. There was a long marble table in the centre piled high with notebooks and stacks of paper and scrolls with scrawls and diagrams on them. Large windows looked out over the gardens at the back of the palace and the mountains beyond. A huge fire burned in the grate, making the room almost unbearably hot.

There was no sign of Nym so Cass wandered over to the bookshelves. She was just perusing the books, which were all about magic, when there was a rustling noise above her. She looked up and gave a start, for there, sitting on a cornice, was a small bright blue bird – a woodland warbler. In a horrible moment of realization, Cass understood that the bird they had thought of as lucky on the journey had in fact been Nym, following them.

The bird flew down and landed softly on the ground where, sure enough, it turned into the magician. She smirked at Cass, delighted by her own cleverness.

"Did you sleep well, Cassandra? Are your quarters comfortable?" she mocked.

"Yes, thank you," Cass replied briskly. "Now, will you please tell me what I'm doing here?"

"I will, but first I want to know how my dear sister is?"

"She's very well. Still the best fortune teller and trancer in Minaris, if that's what you mean?" Cass replied.

Nym broke out into peals of laughter and a self-satisfied smile lit up her face. "Still practising her tiny magic then," she said disdainfully.

There was a pause before Cass said, "So are you going to tell me what I'm doing here?"

"I don't see the harm. You are here, Cassandra, to stop you meddling when things begin."

Cass didn't understand what she meant. "What things?" she asked.

"One of the most important lessons in life is to learn from history – your own and other people's," Nym replied. "As you will know the last Magical Wars were lost largely because of the obtuses.

143

The next one won't be."

"You can't be serious," Cass spluttered. "You're not really going to try to start another Magical War. Look at all the bloodshed, all the lives of ordinary people that were lost."

Nym shrugged. "There are always casualties in such things. I only intend to help Queen Vegna take back what is rightfully hers."

It took Cass a moment to comprehend what she was talking about. "Metrete?" she said. "You are going to try to reclaim Metrete. It will never happen, Nym. The Bundish and the Magical Enforcers won't let it."

"Oh, really?" Nym smirked. "The Veraklian army is every bit as good as the Bundish and I think you'll find that the only decent Magical Enforcers are either imprisoned here or in the Far Lands, thanks to the little disruption my friend Quin is creating there."

That's true, Cass acknowledged with great irritation but she was careful not to show it on her face.

Nym flashed her a self-satisfied smile, adding, "Come the spring, Metrete will be ours again."

"But I'm not the only obtuse," Cass pointed out.

"Obviously not," Nym replied. "And it has taken me a while and a lot of effort to find you all but I think I've managed it now. There is just one young man left in the Far Lands, and an elderly woman in one of the remoter Mid Isles, but I am expecting word any day that they have been dealt with. I have to say, Cassandra, that you have been the most difficult though, since you've become rather good at fighting. Still it's been good for Zirt to be put through his paces."

"Now you have me, what are you going to do with me?" Cass asked, trying to sound as nonchalant as possible.

"You know what, I haven't quite decided," Nym replied. "But I'll let you know when I do."

At that moment, there was a kerfuffle outside the door and it sprung open. A woman appeared who Cass realized was Queen Vegna. She curtsied as best she could while Nym gave a low bow.

The queen was tall and very slender. She had red hair threaded with grey, pinned back by jewelled hairslides. Her face was pinched and tired with violet shadows under her fine green eyes. Her long elegant fingers flashed with heavy rings, but when you looked closely you could see that the nails were bitten down and the skin around her thumbs had been chewed until it was red and raw. Cass could also see that her hands trembled slightly. However, Vegna held herself like a queen, and when she looked at Cass it was with a queen's imperious gaze.

"So, this is Cassandra," she said, examining Cass closely. She had the low gravelly voice of someone who smoked too many cigarillos. "You are only a slip of a thing. I am amazed that you managed to kill the pirate Varen – there must be more to you than meets the eye."

"Cass is skilled with a sword," Nym said with a slight edge to her voice.

Vegna looked thoughtful. "Well, Cassandra, I have business to discuss with Nym." Before Cass could say anything else, Vegna had signalled to the guards and Cass was removed and found herself back in the Slit.

Another Magical War. The thought of it horrified Cass. The Bundish must be warned... But by whom? It wasn't as if she could just send a

146

bird to King Hoff. She could only hope that Idaliz had found out and managed to get out of Veraklia and report back to Lycus.

The days passed and at first all Cass thought about was escape. But after a while, she had to admit that none was possible unless an unexpected opportunity presented itself. The door was entirely solid and locked, the food hatch much too small for her to get through, the window was barred and she had no handy file to saw through them. She had nothing at all that could help her.

Winter deepened and the castle was busy with preparations for the Mid-Winter Feast. *I should be back in Minaris*, Cass thought with sad desperation. *I should be celebrating with Tig, Lin, Mrs Potts and Idaliz, eating snowberry cake and cheering on Dacha's brother in the Ice Race.* But for Cass there was nothing to celebrate.

She would look back on the weeks that followed as one of the toughest times of her life. It wasn't so much the physical hardship, although she was starving and cold much of the time. No, what was really horrendous was the isolation. Her meagre amount of food and firewood was delivered through a hatch, as were clean chamber pots and water. Her only contact with people was the muffled footsteps and voices she heard through her door and the figures she could see from her window. She became obsessed with both.

She listened to the footsteps outside her door and became able to differentiate between the heavy tread of the guards' boots and the lighter ones of the servants. She worked out the times of the patrols and this was how she measured out her days and nights, along with the marks she scratched on the wooden frame of the bed.

The window had a sill just deep enough to sit on and Cass would fold her limbs up and stay there until her legs were screaming with cramp. It looked out over one of the palace's internal courtyards, and she scanned every figure who walked across it, desperately hoping, by some miracle, to see Idaliz. For, Cass reasoned, her friend just might have got a job in the castle to spy on Vegna. But Cass never saw her. She did however get to know the faces of all the servants and courtiers who walked across the square of cobbles, and their routines. She played games with herself about their lives to try and keep her brain amused.

At first Cass practised her physical exercises, keeping herself strong and ready for escape, but she soon found that they gave her so little food that she lacked the energy for them. She had never realized before how quickly you can lose weight and after a couple of weeks her clothes hung off her. It was entirely miserable and it took every inch of Cass's will to stop herself from sinking into a deep depression.

And then after six weeks or so – forty-five days to be precise – something happened. Cass was staring out of the window as usual when she saw a familiar figure sauntering across the courtyard, hands shoved in his pockets. Dacha. He was wearing the palace servants' livery but it was unmistakably him. Her heart beating with shock, Cass shouted his name and banged on the window but he didn't appear to hear her and disappeared into the palace. Cass could have wept with frustration. She scanned the courtyard until it was dark but she didn't see him again. *He must be here for me*, she thought to herself. *He must have come to help me.* Someone must have guessed what had happened – Lin perhaps. But how in the Longest World would he get her out of there?

Late that night, as Cass lay in bed somewhere between sleeping and wakefulness, she heard a noise and something was pushed through the hatch in her door. A cheese pie and a note. It said just two words, written one above the other, *Silence* and *Patience*.

Easy for you to say, she thought with a ghost of a smile as she devoured the pie.

Every day Dacha pushed extra firewood and food through the hatch and Cass began to feel better, mentally and physically. The extra food meant that she could start exercising again and the daily deliveries gave her some hope. She occasionally saw him walking across the courtyard. She stopped herself banging on the glass, but the tiny movement of his head towards her told Cass that he saw her.

However, Cass was also aware that time was marching along. From the notches on her bed frame she counted that she had been there for two and a half months. It was still deepest winter in the mountains but down in Minaris and Bunderland the fierce cold would be loosening its grip and the first signs of spring would be arriving. Nym had said that Vegna would invade in the spring – it could not be far off. *I must try and tell Dacha*, she decided desperately. *He must take word to King Hoff.*

But that night he left her a note, saying, *We go the next night it snows heavily.*

Cass's heart gave a leap of joy. Dacha must have found a way to escape. She could hardly believe it.

It was only a couple of days later when it began to snow in the early evening. An hour had passed when the hatch in her door opened and a pair of sturdy boots and a dagger were shoved in, along with a note. *Midnight – be ready.* Cass felt her spirits soar.

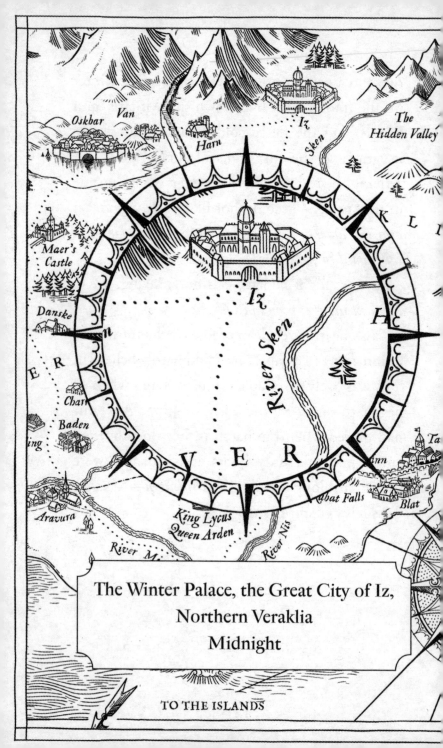

The Winter Palace, the Great City of Iz,
Northern Veraklia
Midnight

TO THE ISLANDS

II

The Escape

Dacha was late. So late that Cass had given up on him coming and was lying back on her bed, dozing in her furs and boots. He slipped quietly into her room. She sat bolt upright, instantly awake and slightly taken aback by his actual presence. She hadn't been so close to another human in over two months. When he hugged her, saying in a whisper, "Where have you gone? There's nothing to you!" Cass couldn't stop herself breaking down into sobs.

"Shh," he said kindly. "You must be quiet, Cass, or we'll be killed before we've even got out of this room."

"Sorry," Cass said, wiping away her tears. "How did you know I was here?"

"I didn't for sure until you banged on the window," he replied. "Lycus sent me – he talked to a friend of yours who, after hearing Arden's story, thought you must be here. Arden and I both knew that we had been bewitched that night."

It must have been Lin, Cass thought and she sent her silent thanks. "Does Lycus also know that Nym and Vegna are planning to invade Metrete? They mean to start another Magical War."

"What?" Dacha exploded, but then quickly said, "We'll have to talk about this later. If we are to go we must leave now before the next lot of guards either notice that the key is missing from their guards' room or pass the door and see it's unbolted. Do you have the dagger?"

Cass nodded.

"Excellent. I think it's safe to assume that we'll both have to do some fighting. We are going to escape via the garden at the rear of the palace." Cass remembered seeing the garden from Nym's room. "There's a door there that gives straight out on to the mountains. Then we need to get

154

ourselves to the woods, where I've hidden some packs and equipment for us. The door is guarded – but only by a couple of palace guards who I'm hoping won't prove too much for you and me. Is that all right?"

"Well, I would prefer to leave in a carriage sledge pulled by white horses," Cass joked. "But under the circumstances I can put up with it."

Dacha gave a snort of laughter.

"Thank you, by the way," Cass said. "For coming to get me, I mean."

"Don't say that yet," he replied. "Wait until we are safely out of here. Come, we must go."

I'd rather die trying to escape than be buried alive here, Cass thought, as she followed him out of the door.

The palace was as quiet as you would expect at three in the morning, with only the patrolling guards and a few night servants around. Dacha had picked a route that took them down the least-used corridors and staircases and luck was on their side. They reached the door to the garden meeting no one.

The garden stretched along the back of the

entire length of the palace and lots of the rooms, like Nym's, had views over it. On the other side of the garden were the stables, dog kennels and some servants' quarters. A cloister ran around its perimeter. This would give them some protection from anyone looking out of their window, but it was patrolled by guards. The mountain door was at the far end of the cloister.

The doorway to the garden was set into a deep arch and Cass and Dacha hid in its darkness until the guards walked past, swinging their lanterns to and fro. Keeping a discreet distance, Cass and Dacha followed them. But they had only gone a little way before they froze.

"Good evening, sire," the guards said to someone ahead. Cass and Dacha looked around for a place to hide but there was nowhere, and besides, whoever was ahead would probably have seen them. Thinking fast, Dacha slung his arm around Cass, pulling her slightly towards him, and started whispering in her ear, as if they were boyfriend and girlfriend. Cass played the part well, giggling and smiling at him.

"Dacha," a voice said. Cass looked at the man

who had greeted him. His expression was one of surprise and anger, and he looked at Cass with distaste.

"Master Ven," Dacha said, immediately letting go of Cass and bowing low.

"What in the Longest World are you doing?" the man spluttered.

Dacha stared at the floor, looking embarrassed. "I was just giving my new friend a tour of the palace," he said, stumbling a little over his words as if he were drunk.

"Is that so?" Master Ven answered, looking at them. "As I'm sure you would be aware if you were sober, such things are strictly forbidden. Come and see me first thing in the morning. Guards!" he called. "Please escort this young man and his friend back to the servants' quarters."

"Yes, sire, I do apologize most sincerely," Dacha said, bowing at his departing figure.

The guards walked over to them. "Who's a naughty boy then?" one of them said to Dacha.

"Me," Dacha replied and then he leaped forwards with his dagger drawn. Cass was only a second later and because of the element of surprise, she could perform a move called 'the sleep chop' on one of the guards. If you hit exactly the right place on the back of someone's neck hard, you can knock them unconscious. She did it perfectly and the guard crumpled to the ground. Dacha's guard wasn't as lucky – Dacha had to use his dagger and the man collapsed in a puddle of blood.

"Right, we need to get out of here now," Dacha said and they sprinted along the corridor back towards the mountain door.

Three guards were there. They looked at Dacha and Cass coming towards them without undue alarm; after all a teenage boy and girl didn't look like the most threatening of enemies. So again the pair had the element of surprise which served them well, at least to start with.

The larger and more burly of the guards headed for Cass while the other two focused on Dacha. The heavy man was a better fighter than Cass was expecting and knew how to use his weight to great effect, nearly flooring Cass. She only just avoided him, landing badly on her wrist. Pain shot through it, but she was back on her feet in a moment, and this time she got him in a hold and scooted his feet out from under him. Reluctant to kill him, she hesitated and that was her mistake. The other guard, seeing his friend in danger, flung himself at Cass, knocking her over and sending her dagger spinning into the air. Both men were back on their feet in a moment.

Look for their weaknesses, Cass said to herself as she faced them. She grabbed her dagger off the floor and waited for them to attack her, which they did. She dodged the heavy man, rounding back on him with her knife and this time she stabbed him hard in the leg. He bellowed with pain and it gave her a moment to push him to the floor, where she could knock him out. The other saw this then turned and ran, shouting for help.

"Grab his sword!" Dacha panted. His guard lay unconscious on the floor and Dacha stripped him quickly of any weapons. "Come, we must fly."

The door opened out on to an expanse of deep snow. A path had been cut through it leading to some woods to the west. "This way," Dacha cried and they sprinted along the path as fast as they could. They had hardly gone any distance when the barking and baying of hunting dogs sang across the silent, snowy landscape. A wave of fear shot through Cass that was so intense she thought she might vomit.

"They've set the dogs on us!" Dacha cried, grabbing Cass's hand and pulling her along even faster. She glanced back to see their dark bodies streaking across the landscape. They were in the woods now and both knew that the dogs would rip them to pieces if they caught them. On and on the pair went, their lungs on fire, using every last piece of strength that they had, surging deeper into the forest. When they thought they had left the hounds behind, they stopped to catch their breath, only to hear the sound of barking seconds away.

Hand in hand they struggled on, knowing the beasts would be on them any moment. Then when all seemed lost, Dacha nearly screamed with relief.

"Here it is!"

Before Cass could say anything Dacha had pulled her over to something – a ladder – and shoved her up on to a wooden platform, pulling himself and the ladder up behind him. He was only just in time. The dogs swarmed below them, snapping and snarling, rearing up on their hind legs. But they couldn't reach them.

"What is this?" Cass asked Dacha, when she had caught her breath.

"It's a huntsman's platform," Dacha replied, nervously watching the dogs below. "I wonder if they will send guards out too?"

"Probably," Cass replied. "But let's wait and see. I'd rather fight them than be ripped to pieces by the dogs."

"Agreed," Dacha replied. And so they waited.

But no one came and the dogs, unable to reach their prey, soon tired. When one hound darted off in another direction after a fox, the others bounded away too. Then a low whistle came through the woods, calling the dogs back to the palace.

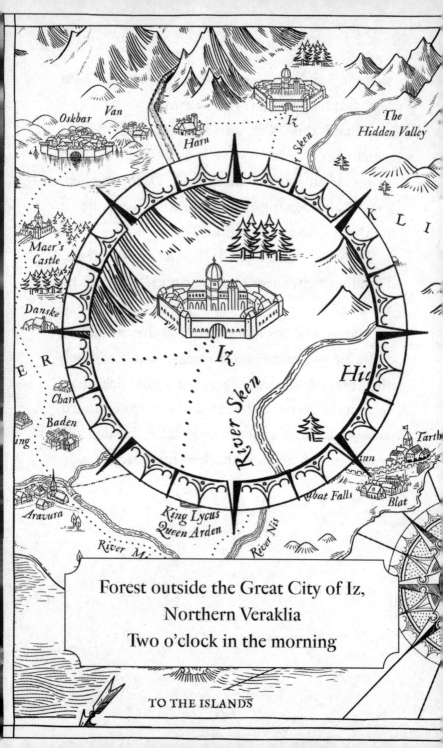

Forest outside the Great City of Iz,
Northern Veraklia
Two o'clock in the morning

TO THE ISLANDS

12

The Hidden Valley

"We must go now. As soon as they realize the dogs haven't got us they'll come after us on horseback," Dacha said, pulling a flask out of his pocket with a shaking hand. He took a long swig from it and passed it to Cass, who did the same, and she felt her nerves steady slightly. Dacha picked up a couple of packs that Cass hadn't noticed and dusted the snow off them.

"I left these here this morning. There's enough food in them for a few days, and tinder. I also packed you a hat and some gloves. Oh, and these." He handed Cass a pair of snowshoes and a staff.

"Well done," Cass replied and took them from

him. "Are we headed to the Bundish border?" she asked as she climbed down the ladder.

"Yes, to Harn. My uncle and aunt live nearby and I have a contact there who smuggled me across the border. Hopefully he should be able to get us out too."

"How were your aunt and uncle?" Cass asked, remembering his concern for them at the Ice Fair.

"Not great," Dacha replied. "I wish they'd leave but it has become almost impossible." He hoisted his pack on to his back. "Anyway, after Harn, we had better go straight to Oskbar to tell King Hoff about Vegna's intention to invade Metrete."

Cass nodded. "That's a good plan, Dacha, but you know Nym is not going to let me go easily," she said with a deep sigh. "She went to a good deal of trouble to capture me in the first place, and now I know about their plans they will do everything in their power to stop me. The dogs are only the beginning."

"I know, Cass," Dacha replied. "But we have to try. Come on, let's get going. It's this way…" He led them along a narrow track that wound its way up into the mountains.

It snowed all morning, at times so fiercely that Cass could only see a metre ahead of her. She had to work hard not to lose her sense of direction as she and Dacha picked their way along the maze of mountain paths. They sought the route with the most cover, through the densest forest and away from any farms or settlements. Perhaps because of the weather, or perhaps by luck, they met no one and the only sounds they heard were the cawing of the snow ravens high above them and the crunch of fresh snow under their shoes.

At around midday, the snowfall stopped and the sky brightened, and through the trees Cass managed to catch glimpses of the snow-drenched valley that they were walking through. They paused to eat a little of the bread that Dacha had brought, at a point where they had a clear view through the trees to the road far below them. It was swarming with palace guards.

"Looking for us," Cass said nervously and Dacha nodded in response.

The sight of the soldiers quickened their feet. The bright weather made the going easier but they were also aware it made them infinitely more visible. Cass's eyes kept darting above them, looking for any glimpse of a woodland warbler. So in some ways they were both pleased when, as the afternoon waned, the weather began to deteriorate again. Heavy clouds closed in, threatening more snow. The light was fading and the temperature, which had never been high, was dropping. Despite their hard marching, Cass was beginning to shiver and her hands and feet were numb with cold.

"I think we should look for somewhere to spend the night and soon, before we get caught in another blizzard," she said to Dacha.

"I agree," he replied. "What do you think we should do? We could camp somewhere in the woods – perhaps we can find a cave or a woodsman's hut. But then we will have to light a fire to stop ourselves freezing to death. Or should we drop down into the valley to find a farm and spend the night with some animals in a barn?"

Cass weighed up the options. "If we light a fire we might as well shout 'here we are!'" she said.

"Not if there's a blizzard, which it looks likely there will be," Dacha pointed out.

"That's true," Cass agreed. "Perhaps that is the

safer option. We could easily be caught if we try to sleep in a barn. What do you think?"

Dacha thought for a moment. "I think we should stay high, it feels less risky. Let's look for somewhere, a cave would be best. It's not as visible and it'll be easier to keep watch."

Cass agreed and they trudged on, keeping their eyes peeled.

About an hour passed and flurries of snow were beginning to fall. Cass was so freezing and exhausted that she would have been happy to just lie down in the snow.

"Let's make camp in the woods," Cass said wearily. "I can't go on much longer."

Dacha turned to her. "No need. Look!" Cass followed his gaze and there, in the murky light, she could see the outline of a hut.

"Oh, thank goodness!" she exclaimed and they lumbered over to it.

Woodsmen's huts were dotted all over the forests of Veraklia and Bunderland and were used not only by the woodsmen and women who worked felling timber in the warmer months, but also by hunters and pig herders. They spent every

167

autumn with their charges, while the animals gorged themselves on the pine nuts and grey velante mushrooms that grew in the mountain forests. The hut was simple with a single window, a small stove, a couple of stools and some bedrolls, but to Dacha and Cass it felt like a palace.

"Look, the last inhabitant has even left us some wood," Dacha exclaimed.

"And tea!" Cass said, picking up a jar from the windowsill and opening it. She inhaled the smell.

"Bitter tea," she said longingly. "I haven't had a cup for months. Not since the fair in Oskbar."

"Let's get a fire going," Dacha said.

"I think we should wait for it to snow more," Cass replied, looking out of the window.

Dacha nodded and eased his pack off his back, and taking off his snowshoes, he unwrapped the bedroll and lay down. He was asleep and snoring in seconds.

"I'll keep watch, shall I?" Cass asked with a laugh. There was no response.

When Dacha woke up an hour later, he found that the hut was deliciously warm and Cass was perched on a stool drinking a cup of tea and looking out of the window. It was dark outside but you could just see by the reflected light from the stove that a snowstorm had blown in.

"It started blizzarding after you went to sleep so I decided I could risk it," she said.

"Good decision!" he said, sitting up and looking cheerful. "Shall we have something to eat? Then I'll keep watch while you get some sleep."

They ate a small but tasty meal of dried meat, chewy dark bread and some dried apricots and drank more bitter tea. But Cass could feel her eyelids beginning to droop.

Dacha noticed and said, "You sleep for a few hours now. I'll keep watch." Cass accepted gratefully and unrolled the other bedroll. She fell asleep in seconds, just as Dacha had done.

"Cass! Wake up! We need to go!" Cass blearily opened her eyes to find Dacha shaking her arm urgently. It took her a few seconds to remember where she was. The fire in the stove was out and she could see the moon through the window.

The snow had cleared.

"I think someone's out there, in the woods. I saw a light, just for a second, like a firefly," Dacha said.

Cass was instantly awake. "Or someone lighting a match for a cigarillo," she replied.

"Exactly," he said.

Cass sprang up and pulled on her boots. Snowshoes were no good if you were in a hurry so she shoved them in her pack, along with her hat and gloves. She pulled on her coat, refastened her sword and scabbard around her waist and slung the pack on her back. Dacha was standing to the side of the window, looking out. "I don't know if I imagined it but I think I just saw something move in those trees."

"Come on, let's get out of here," Cass said.

But as she spoke someone kicked in the door.

The hut was so small that only one person could come in at a time and this worked to Cass and Dacha's advantage – they dispatched the first two figures with ease. But their two comrades were not going to make the same mistake. They waited for Dacha and Cass to tentatively walk out of the door before they pounced.

There was just enough light for a sword fight, the blades catching the moonlight, but Cass could hardly make out the face of the person attacking her. It was only when she had defeated him that she saw he was a boy about the same age as her. *I'm sorry*, she said in her head.

"They're soldiers, not palace guards," Dacha said in a low voice.

"Do you think they were a random patrol?" Cass asked.

Dacha sighed. "I'd like to think that, but I suspect that they were looking for us." He paused before saying, "Come on, we should get going."

It was still several hours until dawn, but Cass and Dacha's eyes soon adapted to the darkness. They went warily, trying to keep to the densest parts of the forest, but it wasn't long before they saw another group of soldiers huddled round a fire. Cass and Dacha picked their way silently above them, but quickly came across yet another group. As soon as they were clear of that lot, the pair stopped for a whispered conversation.

"This is hopeless," Dacha said. "The woods are

swarming with soldiers and once the light comes in a couple of hours it will be impossible for us to avoid them." He sighed and rubbed his tired eyes. His voice was full of defeat. "I've been stupid to bring us this way. To head to Harn is the obvious thing to do."

"But what other option is there? We need to warn King Hoff," Cass replied.

"We can't warn him if we are dead."

"True. Do you want to head into the Northern Wastes? We could perhaps hide there. Or what about the Citadel of the Mountain Sisters? Could we claim sanctuary with them?"

Dacha shook his head. "The Mountain Sisters are too connected to the queen – they would hand us over immediately. If we head north then we are quickly into mining country and there is nothing there but snow, ice wolves and slave gangs. The cold is even more brutal and it will be impossible to find anything to eat or anywhere to stay."

"What about heading down to Naz instead?" Cass asked. Naz was another border town, about twenty miles south of Harn.

"Possibly," he replied, weighing it up. "But I

know no one in Naz. How will we begin to find someone to take us across the border?"

"There will be some way I'm sure. We won't know unless we try," Cass said, trying to sound as optimistic as she could.

So they headed south, picking their way carefully down the valleys. The dawn broke, which helped them a little as they could see where the soldiers were by the trails of smoke that their fires made. The woods were indeed crawling with men. They had a couple of near misses later in the morning once the soldiers were on the move but luck was on their side again and, by midday, they were seeing fewer patrols. They pushed themselves on and in the late afternoon they dropped down into lower country where they passed a few isolated farms.

As they knew there was no question of a fire, when night had fallen and they could bear the cold no more they crept into a barn where they spent a freezing, uncomfortable night with a herd of noisy sheep for company. They woke again as early as they could and walked on, trying to ignore the bitter cold, eager to put as many miles as they could between themselves and the soldiers.

In the mid-afternoon, as the light was beginning seep away, they took a steep, rocky path that led them down into a narrow, secluded valley.

"I think this is the Hidden Valley," Dacha said, looking around him. "Which means we have come too far east." He sighed.

Cass was fighting great waves of exhaustion. "Never mind. Let's find somewhere to spend the night before it gets dark and then we can double back in the morning and head west."

"I hear there's a fine inn just down the valley – it's famous for its delicious stew and noodles," Dacha joked.

Cass laughed. "If only…" she replied when suddenly something hurtled through the air from above, covering both of them. It took Cass a moment to realize that it was a net. She immediately went to draw her dagger but before she could, she felt the sharp point of a sword against her neck and a voice said in a strong Veraklian accent, "Neither of you move."

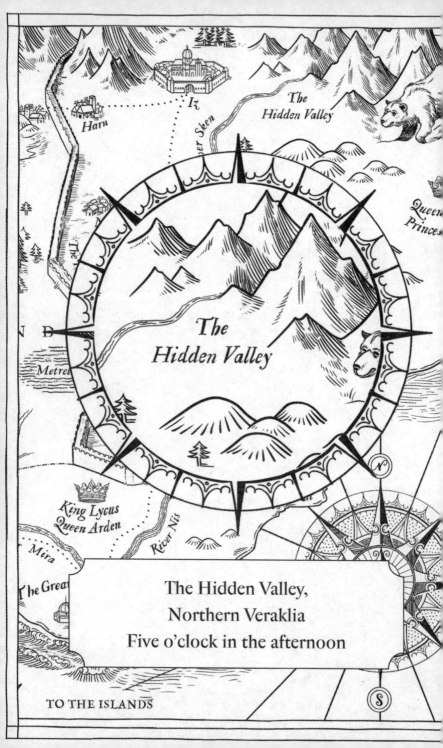

The Hidden Valley,
Northern Veraklia
Five o'clock in the afternoon

13

Sir Drex

The net was ripped off and several figures surrounded them. Seven, Cass quickly counted, including the two that had swords pointed at Dacha and her. They all had scarves over their faces like the Sins and shepherds' hats pulled low over their brows so Cass couldn't tell whether they were men or women. But they were clearly not soldiers or palace guards.

"Who are you?" one of the figures asked Cass and Dacha.

"Just travellers," Dacha replied as casually as he could with a sword at his throat.

"There are no travellers in Veraklia, not these

days. So you'll need to do better than that."

Whoever these people are, Cass thought, *they are outlaws or bandits of some description and unlikely to be friends of the queen. But perhaps there will be a price on our heads that will tempt them to hand us over?* Cass weighed it up in her mind. The men hadn't gone straight for their wallets, which suggested they weren't robbers so perhaps any reward wouldn't be of any interest.

"Come on, who are you?" the voice insisted and the pressure of the sword tip on Cass's throat increased. She decided to take a chance.

"We have escaped from the palace at Iz," Cass replied.

Dacha threw her a look clearly saying, *Are you crazy?*

"Really," the voice said, sounding interested. "Well, you'd better come with us then."

Before they knew what was happening they were blindfolded and gagged and their hands were bound. Cass felt her arms being grabbed tightly and she was marched off through the woods.

It was hard to tell how far they walked but Cass reckoned it was only about half a mile. They appeared to go down and then up and she heard an owl hoot and some other animal calls but nothing gave her any real clue which direction they were being taken in.

Then abruptly they came to a stop and a voice next to her said, "You have to climb a ladder now. Here's the first rung," and her hands were placed on a wooden rung.

Cass did as she was told and climbed up about three metres of ladder. She was then grabbed by two sets of arms and lifted on to something. *Am I in a tree house?* she wondered but when she walked, the ground beneath her felt too solid – more like stone. She was led on and up another ladder, and then quite suddenly the air became much warmer and she heard the crackling noise of a fire. She was stopped by whoever was leading her and her blindfold and gag were removed, although her hands remained bound.

Cass found herself standing next to Dacha beside a fire pit in a large cave. It was decorated like a normal room with tables and chairs and rugs but the walls were covered in ancient-looking paintings of stick men and animals that drew

Cass's eye like a magnet. She had to tear herself away from them to focus on the two men on the other side of the room. They were having a whispered conversation. It ended and one man went and stood by the cave's entrance while the other came forwards saying, "Welcome."

He was in his sixties, Cass estimated, but he held himself with the strength and vigour of a younger man. His face was very lined but his hair was still thick and more red than white, and he regarded her and Dacha with a curious, intelligent gaze. Dacha shifted slightly next to Cass, giving her the impression that he knew the man.

"Is it true that you two escaped from the palace?" he asked. "That is quite an achievement."

"It is true," Cass replied. "I was a prisoner there and my friend helped me escape."

"So that is why the mountains are crawling with soldiers. You are obviously very precious," he said, looking at Cass with interest. "Why was Vegna holding you prisoner?"

"Because I'm an obtuse," Cass answered.

The man raised his eyebrows and then thought for a moment. "Of course, you would be very dangerous for that witch, Nym." He said the name with disgust.

"And you," he turned to Dacha. "Did you just happen to be there?"

"Something like that, sire," Dacha replied with a polite smile.

"You recognize me do you, young man?"

"I do, Sir Drex. But like everyone else, I thought you were in the Islands."

The man smiled. "That sounds a good deal warmer. No, I could not leave Veraklia. I have stayed with my band of loyal supporters and this way I can do something to ease the lives of those in the area suffering under the queen's tyranny. Well, as you know about me, I think you can do me the courtesy of telling me a little about yourselves. You first, young man. What's your name?"

"It's Dacha," he replied.

"A good Veraklian name," he said with a smile. "So, Dacha, how did you come to help a Minarian girl escape from the Winter Palace?"

Dacha hesitated. Sir Drex said, "As you know, Dacha, I am no friend of the queen's so do not fear I will hand you over to her. But I have to know if I can trust you."

"You can trust me," Dacha replied. "But I am part of the Queen's Guard in Minaris and I was sent by Queen Arden and King Lycus to try to rescue Cass."

"I see," he said, considering this. "You are from Minaris?"

"Yes, my parents moved there when I was a baby," Dacha replied.

"As you know, historically I am no friend of King Lycus's but he has been more than helpful to Princess Taryn. And certainly I don't wish you any harm for working for him," Sir Drex said and then turned to Cass. "Who are you, young lady, that you have such powerful friends?"

"My name is Cass and I was working as a lady-in-waiting for the queen when Nym captured me."

Sir Drex nodded, satisfied with the answer. "I see," he said. "Important enough to rescue but not important enough to start a war over. So how exactly did you escape?" he asked. "We both know that it is not an easy thing."

"I stole the key from the guards' room and then we fought our way out," Dacha replied. "We were lucky."

Sir Drex raised his eyebrows. "You were," he said with a half-smile. She could see him weighing up in his mind whether to question them more, and deciding not to. Instead he asked, "And where are you headed now? Are you hoping to cross the border somewhere?"

"My plan was to cross at Harn – that's where I came in. But there were too many soldiers to go that way so we have come south instead. We thought we might cross at Naz," Dacha replied.

"I'm afraid there's no chance there at all. To be truthful it will be almost impossible anywhere. The borders are entirely closed and constantly patrolled by soldiers. Besides, Vegna's spies are everywhere. Everyone is hungry and it takes a strong man or woman not to sell a secret."

"Sire, I feel we must tell you something," Cass interjected. "Something that you may already know perhaps."

"Go on," he said.

"The queen and Nym are planning to invade Metrete. It is Nym's intention to start another Magical War."

Sir Drex paused before answering. "I knew it was

an ambition of Vegna's so it doesn't surprise me. And it makes sense of the massive barracks that she has constructed in Enzit. So you will warn the Bundish if you get across somehow?"

"I cannot stand by and do nothing while Nym starts something that may cause the deaths of hundreds of people," Cass said. "In the last Magical War, thousands died—"

"I know, Cass, I remember," he interrupted her.

"Sorry, sire," Cass said.

A young man appeared with a tray of food that he put down on the table. "Let me think about all you have said. In the meantime, can I offer you something to eat?" Sir Drex asked.

Cass and Dacha agreed and the young man took off the ropes around their wrists. They sat down as Sir Drex poured them each a glass of winter wine and served them a plate of lamb stew and noodles, which, remembering Dacha's comment about the inn down the valley, made Cass smile to herself.

Cass's eyes were again drawn to the wall paintings. They were simple drawings, like a child's, of animals and human figures, but they had a magic and beauty about them that Cass loved. "Sir Drex, please would you tell me who drew these paintings?"

Sir Drex paused in his eating and looked at the walls around him, smiling slightly. "They are beautiful, aren't they?" he said. "I believe they were drawn more than a thousand years ago by the first Veraklians, who must have made their homes in these caves."

"Really?" Cass replied, her imagination caught. She tried to picture such people. "I wonder how they lived? What they wore?"

"I cannot help you with any of that, I'm afraid, but what I can show is that, if you look over there, you will see those figures with wings. Even then we were obsessed with flying and the sky! Let me help you to some more stew."

After supper, Cass and Dacha were shown to a small room, or cave to be more accurate, with two beds and, tellingly, a guard stationed outside. Sir Drex clearly did not trust them entirely.

"Do you think he will do anything to help us stop Vegna?" Cass asked Dacha as they were falling asleep.

"I don't know," he replied truthfully.

The pair were woken up in what they both guessed to be the early morning – it was hard to tell time in the cave – by a guard with some bread and tea, and told that Sir Drex wished to see them.

"My guards have reported that there were soldiers in the valley overnight, presumably looking for you. They have moved on now – returning to the Falling Valley hopefully," Sir Drex announced when they joined him.

Cass and Dacha nodded in response, taking in what he said.

"You are safe here," he continued. "Which is why I was going to offer you the option of staying with us. I could always use good fighters and you can help me with my work, which is focused on easing the suffering of the everyday people and making life a little more uncomfortable for Vegna."

It's a good offer, Cass thought, a kind offer, and a sensible one for them to take. They could stay there hidden until Vegna invaded Metrete, and then perhaps with so many soldiers involved in that campaign, or the general chaos on that border, it would be easier to sneak across. Yet... Cass felt she must at least try to tell the Bundish of Vegna's plans. And, more selfishly, she desperately wanted to go home. She glanced over to Dacha to see his reaction.

"Why don't I give you a few minutes to discuss it?" Sir Drex said and walked out of the room, leaving them alone.

"What do you think?" Cass asked Dacha.

"I think it would be the most sensible thing to do," Dacha replied.

Cass's heart sank and it obviously showed on her face because Dacha said with a rueful smile, "But it's not what you want to do, is it, Cass?"

She sighed and shook her head. "You could stay," she said. "And I will continue on my own."

"Of course I'm not going to let you do that," he replied.

"I'll be fine," Cass protested. "It's easier for one person to slip through in some ways. I can look after myself."

Dacha ran his hands through his hair and said, "No, Cass, you are right – we must try to get word to the Bundish. Also Lycus sent me here to get you and bring you back to Minaris. Those were my orders so that is what I should do."

Sir Drex came back in. "So have you made a decision?"

Cass spoke. "It is very kind of you, but we feel we should press on and try to cross the border."

Sir Drex smiled to himself. "I thought you would say that," he replied. "And I admire you in some ways, although I think you are foolhardy. It will be very dangerous; Nym is a formidable enemy."

"I know," Cass replied.

"Well, if that's what you want so be it," Sir Drex said. "My offer stands if you change your minds and if not I wish you good luck."

"Thank you, sire," they both replied.

Cass and Dacha presumed the interview was over but then Sir Drex said, "I've got another idea. I had intended to send a couple of men down to Enzit today, as I have to get a message to a friend there."

Enzit, Cass knew vaguely, was a city to the south, at the head of the Lake of Forgiveness.

"It is a long way by foot but by slip boat it is only three days' journey. You are only twenty miles from the border there and you have as good a chance of getting across there as anywhere."

"But is the River Sken not still frozen?" Dacha asked.

"No. Only yesterday, I sent my men down to the bottom of the valley where the river becomes navigable to check, and they said the ice had melted just enough to allow a slip boat down. So what if I were to lend you a couple of such boats and in return you would deliver a letter? Does that sound like a fair bargain to you?"

Cass and Dacha exchanged glances and Cass replied, "It does."

"Good. A couple of my men will escort you down to the boats and give you instructions as to where to leave them." He went over to a desk and picked up a letter in a sealed envelope.

"Here it is," he said, handing it to Cass. "Guard it well. The address to take it to is Number Seven, Street of Sails, not far from the lakefront. You must be sure to give it only into the hands of the mistress of the house, a woman named Masha."

Cass nodded and put the letter in the inside pocket of her coat. She and Dacha thanked Sir Drex.

"Goodbye and good luck," he replied. "May we meet in happier times."

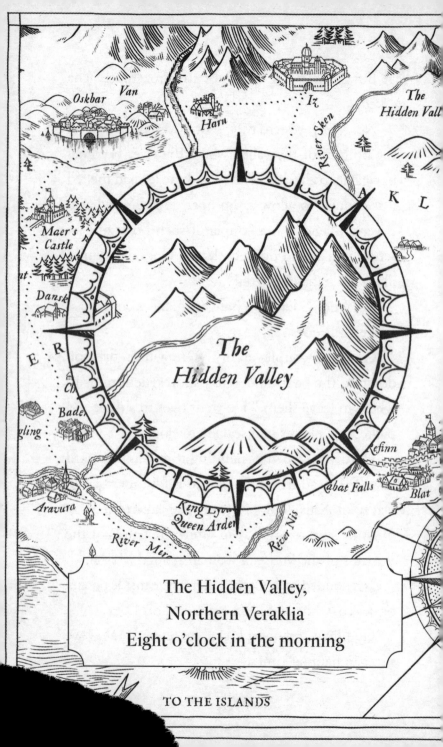

The Hidden Valley,
Northern Veraklia
Eight o'clock in the morning

TO THE ISLANDS

14

Down the River Sken

Blindfolded again but this time with their hands free, Dacha and Cass were taken out, down the ladders, and into the fresh air. They were given their bags back and with someone leading them, they followed a path down the valley until they came to the river.

They stopped and had their blindfolds removed, finding that they had left the Hidden Valley and had come down into a larger, wider valley with a river meandering through it. The water was still frozen at the edges but in the centre there was a channel of free-flowing water about a metre and a half across.

They walked a little away along the riverbank until they came to a small wooden boat hut. The men accompanying them brought out two slip boats – light and narrow, carved from the trunk of a single tree. Cass had seen them before in the Islands but she had never been in one and eyed them nervously.

The men set the boats down on the ground and one of them explained, "You need to be careful getting in as the ice near the channel will be thin, so I suggest you smash as much of it away as you can. I know the channel is narrow but it should be broad enough for you to manage and hopefully as you get lower down it will widen. The currents are strong in some places but they are good boats, I'm sure they will serve you well. But just a word of warning – if there is a sudden thaw up in the mountains then the river will quickly flood and be very dangerous. There is a tent in one of the canoes that you can use to camp, and here is some food." He handed them a bag.

"Thank you so much," Cass said.

"Thank you," echoed Dacha. "Where should we leave the boats?"

The other man spoke up. "When you get to the outskirts of Enzit there's a boathouse on the left, painted red. It's owned by a man named Bois. Leave the boats with him. Good luck." Cass and Dacha thanked them profusely again and bid them farewell.

When the men had gone they both looked at the slip boats and looked at each other. "Ever been in one of these?" Dacha asked Cass.

"No," Cass admitted.

"Me neither," he replied with a laugh. "But how hard can it be?"

Cass looked at the boats. "Quite hard, I suspect."

They soon found that getting in the boats was tricky but after that it was relatively straightforward. Once Cass had got used to how low the boat sat in the water, and realized that it wasn't about to tip her out into its freezing depths, she relaxed slightly. And after an hour or so she was actively enjoying floating down the icy blue water as it wound its way between the deserted, snowy mountains, putting a satisfying distance between them and Zirt and his soldiers. The boats slid gracefully but quickly downstream and they only needed to use their paddles occasionally for steering. The sun came out and for the first time in months Cass felt like she could breathe a little more freely.

They came up to some rapids as the light was fading and as they had had to go through the palaver of taking the boats out of the water and carrying them down the steep path by the falls, they decided to make camp in the woods by the river then and there. They assembled the tiny tent and set about making a fire.

"We're twenty miles away from the soldiers," Dacha pointed out. "Our chief dangers now are the cold and mountain wolves and bears, and the only protection against them is fire."

Could we really have outrun Zirt so easily? Cass wondered but she also knew that Dacha was right about the wild animals. They needed a fire. So after a bit of rootling around they found some reasonably dry wood and some twigs and pine cones for kindling. Soon they had it going and they ate some of the food that Sir Drex's men had given them.

"First or second watch?" Dacha asked her.

Cass felt wide awake. "I'll stay up now, you sleep."

Dacha yawned. "Thank you."

Cass sat peacefully by the fire, feeding it wood and watching as the day was whittled away into evening and then darkened into night. There was a spectacular sunset somewhere behind her but Cass was happy observing the different shades of blue in the sky above her and spotting the stars as they came out. The moon appeared, a broad slice of silver in the sky that reflected off the snow and the mountains around, gently illuminating the running water of the river. Pine owls started to call up in the trees around her and, to her delight, she watched a family of beavers appear and frolic around on the riverbank. It was a moment of peaceful solitude and Cass was almost sorry when Dacha woke up. But he saw the beavers too and, anxious not to disturb them, he came and sat next to her quietly. They watched them together in silence until the animals retreated back into their nest.

"I'm guessing that as a Veraklian you know all about the stars," Cass said, gazing at the sky above her, which was a mass of pinpricks of light. "I don't think I have ever seen so many, even out in the Islands, and I can never remember their names."

Dacha laughed. "Yes, I had a good Veraklian education in the stars. My father used to take me up to the roof on most clear nights to show me the different constellations and teach me their names. The easiest one to pick out is over there – the goat," he said, pointing up to a collection of stars to the north. "Do you see those two particularly bright stars? Those are the top of its horns and then can you trace down its nose?"

It took Cass a moment before she could see what he was talking about. "Oh yes!" she cried. "Show me more. Where is the constellation of the bear? Mrs Potts was always trying to point it out to me and I could never see it."

"That is over in the east – can you see those four stars all together? That's its nose…" Then he went silent. He touched Cass's arm and pointed to a large shape moving down by the river.

"Talking of bears," he whispered to her. And he shifted over to grab a couple of the branches from the pile of wood they had amassed. He put one end of each in the fire to heat them up to frighten the bear away if it came over.

Cass knew that Veraklian mountain bears might look cuddly with their thick brown fur coats but they were every bit as aggressive and vicious as ice wolves. They watched tensely as the bear smashed the ice in the river and drank from it. He stayed by the water for a while and then lumbered off along the bank.

"He's gone," Dacha announced. "But I'll stay up in case he returns. You must get some sleep."

Cass nodded gratefully and curled up by the fire, sleeping soundly for a few hours.

The following day dawned bright and clear again, though bitterly cold. The River Sken flowed on, cutting its way through the steep valleys of the mountain uplands. Rocky outcrops and forest lined the valley sides – there was no fertile grazing land so few people chose to live there. They only passed a handful of isolated woodsmen's houses with blue smoke twirling up to the sky and they appeared to go unnoticed except for once, when a dog idly wandering along the shore barked furiously at them.

They made good progress and when they stopped to camp that night, Dacha estimated that they had covered more than a hundred miles since they had left. "If tomorrow is the same we will have nearly reached Enzit," Dacha announced.

They passed an uneventful night but woke to heavy skies and snow. However, the snow, although steady, didn't hinder them in any way. In fact it added to their sense of cocooning and isolation. They saw no one and at some points she could have believed that they were the only people alive in the Longest World.

But the snow meant that what little light there was had all but gone by mid-afternoon and they were forced to stop and camp earlier than they would have liked. Dacha cursed the spring snow, which had made everything so damp that he struggled to find dry firewood and they only managed a meagre fire. They passed a cold, damp night and woke feeling disgruntled. The day promised to be as miserable weather-wise as the one before.

"Shall we risk an inn in Enzit?" Dacha asked Cass as they set off. "I have silvers."

The threat of Zirt had receded in her mind and images of baths, feather beds and hot meals danced around her head. "Yes, please," she said. "How far away are we?"

"I think we should reach there about midday," Dacha replied.

As they neared Enzit, the foothills of the mountains softened and broadened into hills, and the spell of isolation was broken by the appearance of farms and hamlets, and bridges bisected the river. It was also, Cass noticed, slightly warmer. The snow was starting to melt, revealing patches of dull brown earth. Cass could even see wild icepearl flowers poking up in places. *Spring*, she thought with a bittersweet jolt, as she considered Nym and Vegna's plans to invade Metrete.

An hour later they reached the outskirts of Enzit. They spotted the red boathouse easily enough and although there was no one around they left the boats there, along with the camping equipment and a note of thanks. Then, with a feeling of trepidation, they made their way towards the city walls of Enzit.

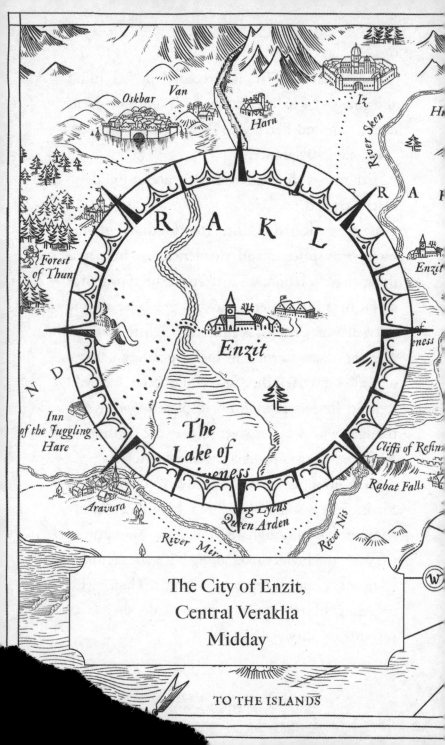

Oskbar

Van

Harn

Iz

River Skeen

H

R A

H

Enzit

R A K L

Forest
of Thun

Enzit

ness

Inn
of the Juggling
Hare

The
Lake of
iveness

Cliffs of Refin

Rabat Falls

Aravura

g Lycus
Queen Arden

N D

River Mir

River Nis

The City of Enzit,
Central Veraklia
Midday

W

TO THE ISLANDS

15

A Change of Plan

On the outskirts of the city, just before they entered the walls, they passed the army barracks that Sir Drex had referred to. At the sight of it Dacha let out a low whistle. "That's enormous. There must be five thousand men in there."

The sight of it made Cass nervous. "Come on," she urged. "Let's get away from it."

There was no queue to enter the city and the gatekeeper looked at them with interest. "We're from Iz. We've come to see our aunt," Dacha said, putting on a mountain accent.

"Is that right?" The man looked sly and dishonest, Cass thought, and sure enough he said,

"I sometimes have great difficulty believing stories unless I have a few silvers to help them seem more convincing."

"How many silvers?" Dacha asked.

"I would say ten in your case – each," he said. It was an astronomical amount of money but Dacha made no objection. He just fished the coins out of his pocket and handed them over to the gatekeeper.

"Good doing business with you," the man said and nodded them through.

"Shall we head straight to the Street of Sails?" Dacha asked when they were out of earshot.

Cass nodded. "Yes, but if we see anywhere selling food can we get some? I'm starving."

Dacha laughed. "I agree."

Enzit had been a beautiful, wealthy and bustling city, blessed in its situation at the head of the Lake of Forgiveness and the intersection of the roads coming from Iz in the north, Minaris in the south and Metrete in the east. Just before Enzit, the River Sken split into a hundred smaller streams, forming a delta, which Enzit had been built on and which gave it its nickname City of a Hundred Bridges. It was also home to a huge number of gold traders who had spent generously on strong city walls, attractive civic buildings and a long, broad lakeside promenade. They had built themselves magnificent mansions and splendid summer houses along the shores of the lake. But all that was in happier times and a very different scene greeted Cass and Rip.

The snow had almost gone from the city but that somehow heightened its depressing appearance. The streets themselves were largely deserted save for a few pitiful, starving cats and some gangs of beggar children. The adults they did see looked to Cass to be heavily enchanted. The windows of many houses were shuttered but Cass felt as if behind them were eyes watching them as they wandered along, hopelessly lost in the maze of claustrophobic, winding alleys and hidden squares, hoping to stumble upon the Street of Sails.

Without warning, the passageway they were in turned a corner and they found themselves on the promenade overlooking the lake. Here there were a few people, mostly crowded around a magician, their faces heavy and stupid.

"Don't look!" Cass warned Dacha, who was

staring at him. "He's powerful – he has them all in his thrall."

Dacha blinked and tore his eyes away with some difficulty.

"Come," said Cass firmly taking his hand. "There's some food here."

She led him over to a tatty stall selling some grey-looking vegetable pies.

"These could certainly do with a bit of magic," she joked.

"I'm so hungry I'll eat anything," Dacha said and he gave the woman the exorbitant amount of coins she wanted for a couple of pies.

They ate them sitting on a bench that overlooked the lake, their backs to the magician. It was still frozen enough for a few people to be skating on the ice. Cass took a bite of the pie. It was tasteless and had an unpleasant, grainy texture. "I'm only eating this this because I'm starving," she announced.

"It's really pretty disgusting," Dacha replied cheerfully, shovelling the pie into his mouth.

The watery sun was trying to come out and Cass felt just a touch of warmth in it. She shut her eyes and leaned back against the hard wood of the bench.

"I am going to have to have another one of those revolting pies," Dacha said, getting up.

"Remember to avoid the magician," she called after him as she continued to watch the skaters on the ice.

Then, moments later, she heard a voice that chilled her blood. It was a man singing, "Oh, I'm the Queen of Minaris, All the ladies have to curtsy to me…"

Cass spun around to see Zirt, flanked by soldiers, smirking at her.

"Kitten!" he greeted her. Cass could see Dacha behind them and without a moment's pause, she ran. How she dodged them she would never know but she did, and with Dacha by her side she pelted along the promenade.

Not knowing where they were heading, they randomly took turnings, their only thought to get away from Zirt and his soldiers. But Cass and Dacha were at a great disadvantage, for they had no knowledge of the layout of the city and all its tricks and deceptions. Cass quickly realized that the whole place was enchanted. Twice she had to pull Dacha away from careering down obvious dead ends that would have trapped them instantly, and then he was sure that they should take a left turn which Cass could see would lead them straight back to the soldiers.

"Oh no, they've separated," Cass panted as she glimpsed three soldiers charging across a bridge ahead of them. "And we can't go back, Zirt is behind us." She looked around. There was a narrow court through an arch that looked like it led away from both groups. "This way," she said, yanking Dacha along.

But unfortunately the court led back into a small courtyard where the three soldiers they had seen on the bridge were waiting, swords drawn.

"Got you!" one of them sneered as Cass and Dacha threw their packs on the floor and pulled their swords out of their sheaths.

The fight began. Two of the three soldiers took on Cass, while Dacha had just one, but he was the best fighter. In fact, they were all good, Cass quickly realized, no doubt hand-picked by Zirt himself. Cass and Dacha fought well but they were making no headway and Cass could feel herself beginning to panic, thinking that Zirt and the other soldiers would be there any moment and then the whole thing would be over.

Focus! she instructed herself but she could feel the fight turning against her and the effort of fending off two blades rather than one defeating her. Then Dacha gave a cry. He was injured but Cass couldn't see how badly. He was still holding his sword but he was struggling. Cass's confidence faltered, which was disastrous and one of the soldiers knocked her sword out of her hand, sending it clattering across the courtyard. The two soldiers gave shouts of victory and one held his sword to Cass's neck as the other joined in the fight against Dacha. He fought bravely but only seconds later he too had his sword on the ground and a blade at his neck.

"Our boss is going to be pleased to see you two," one of the men said as they pulled ropes out of their pockets to tie Cass and Dacha up.

Then with no warning, a voice from above them cried, "Not so fast!" and a figure jumped down from the roof, landing neatly on the ground in front of them.

The soldiers were so surprised they made the mistake of all turning to face the person, giving Cass and Dacha the opportunity to dive for their dropped swords.

Despite the dark clothes and a mask, Cass recognized the figure instantly and her heart leaped with joy. It was her friend, Idaliz.

Together they made short work of the soldiers.

"Quickly!" Idaliz cried as soon as they were done. "Come now!" she instructed and they followed her down the passageway off the square that the soldiers must have come along. About halfway along she pushed on a solid-looking door. It opened and they all dived inside. Idaliz shut it behind them and pulled the bolts across.

"What were you doing on the roof?" Cass spluttered as soon as they were safely in the hall of the house.

"It's the best way to get around without being seen. But never mind that, what in the Longest World are you two doing in Enzit?" Idaliz cried, pulling off her mask and hood to reveal her smiling, freckled face and long auburn hair.

"Dacha, you should be in Minaris looking after the queen, and Cass, I expected you to be halfway to the Far Isles by now!"

"It's a long story," Cass replied, grinning from ear to ear. It was Idaliz! She couldn't believe their luck. "Why have you not returned to Minaris?"

"I haven't been able to get back. I—"

At that moment, the street outside was full of shouting and running feet. "Soldiers!" Idaliz whispered. "Come this way!" She led them along a narrow hall and into a room at the back of the house, where a man and a woman were studying a large map spread out on a table.

There was a fierce banging on the front door.

"Masha, Riven, I need to hide these two," Idaliz murmured. "The soldiers are after them."

They quickly moved the table and whipped back the carpet, revealing a trapdoor. "Don't make a sound," Masha advised as she hustled them down a ladder and into a tiny dark space. The trapdoor was shut and there was the sound of moving furniture, muffled voices and heavy footsteps. Cass focused on trying to slow down her breathing as it was coming in ragged, terrified blasts.

After what seemed like about half an hour, but was probably only a few minutes, they heard the voices and the footsteps recede. After a brief pause, there was more shuffling of furniture and the trapdoor opened. Idaliz's face appeared.

"They've gone," she said and helped them up and out of the hiding place. "Masha, Riven, these are my friends, Cass and Dacha."

"It's good to meet you," Riven said. He was a tall thin man, with a thoughtful face.

Masha, who Cass took for his wife, said, "You are most welcome. Any friends of Idaliz's are friends of ours."

Masha. That was the name that Sir Drex had said! Cass remembered. "I don't suppose this is Number Seven, Street of Sails, is it?" Cass asked.

Riven and Masha looked at Cass quizzically. "It is," Masha replied. "Why?"

Cass pulled the letter out of her pocket. "It's from Sir Drex," she explained and she handed it to Masha who opened it.

"Have you come from him?" Riven asked, surprised.

"Yes," Dacha replied. "He gave us shelter when

we'd escaped from the Winter Palace."

"You escaped from the Winter Palace!" Idaliz exclaimed. "Come, you must tell us all."

"I'll make some tea," Riven said. "It sounds like a story that deserves it."

They all helped rearrange the furniture and then sat around the table. Riven appeared with a large metal teapot and poured them bowls of bitter tea.

"So, Cass, Dacha, let's hear your story," Idaliz said.

"You tell it, Cass," Dacha said. And so she did – she told the entire tale from her first sight of Zirt's accomplice in the inn at Aravura, to her capture in Oskbar by Nym and her imprisonment in the Winter Palace, and then her rescue by Dacha and their journey down the mountains.

"Do you know," Dacha said, "of Vegna and Nym's terrible plans to invade Metrete?"

Masha, Riven and Idaliz all sighed, exchanging glances. "Yes, I'd found that out," Idaliz replied. "I have been desperately trying to get across to Metrete for the last month or so to warn Taryn and King Hoff but it has proved impossible. Until now," she added.

"You're going?" Cass asked, excited. "You've found a way?"

"How? Can we come?" Dacha said eagerly.

Idaliz shook her head. "You know I would take you if I could but I'm afraid it's out of the question." When she saw their faces fall, she explained. "There's one cart allowed over the Bundish border every week laden with luxury goods for the palace at Iz. It's driven by a Veraklian trader and he has agreed, after considerable persuasion, to take me tomorrow, hidden in the small space under his seat. There's barely room for me, let alone another two people, I'm afraid."

"Is there anyone else who might take us across?" Dacha asked.

"Not that I know of," Riven replied. "Getting across the border is almost impossible."

"Is there really no way?" Cass asked, feeling a great cloud of hopelessness descending upon her.

"You might be best going back to Sir Drex," Masha said.

The very thought of turning around and trekking back up to the mountains made Cass want to weep with frustration.

"The only other option you could try is the very far south," Riven said. "It is just possible that with all the troops going to Metrete there will be fewer soldiers on the Minarian border and perhaps you might be able to cross somewhere there."

Cass thought of what she knew about the southern border of Veraklia with Minaris. The two countries were separated by a geographical phenomenon known as the Cliffs of Refinn, a steep rock face a thousand metres high. The most spectacular part of them was the Razat Falls – an enormous set of waterfalls where all the water from the Lake of Forgiveness tumbled over the edge of the cliffs. Cass had been to see them many years before and the sight of the white water thundering down from the sky had made a great impression on her.

"You are not suggesting we go over the falls in a barrel, are you?" Dacha asked with a nervous laugh. There had been stories in the news sheets of Veraklian refugees desperate to reach Minaris who had done so, often with terrible consequences.

"It might be your only option." Riven smiled. "But before you do, you should look at the border crossings at Blat and Tarth." They were the two places where, over thousands of years, rivers had carved narrow valleys that dropped down to the same level as Minaris.

Dacha sighed. "But it's miles to get down to the south and too dangerous to go along the road."

Masha nodded. "The most sensible way would be to skate down the Lake of Forgiveness."

"Will the ice hold?" Cass asked. "The ice was melting on the River Sken even up in the mountains."

"It depends on the weather but the lake ice is always the last to melt because it's such a large mass of water," Masha replied.

"And if it does, you can always walk along the shore," Riven pointed out. "You should be safe enough doing that – the villages there are very isolated. The road and lake only come together at one point at the village of Wyza. If you push yourselves you can probably cover twenty miles a day, in which case it will take you about ten days. I know a woman, Dorcas, who is a seamstress in Balzen, the town at the end of the lake, which is very near the border. She will help you if she can."

"What do you think?" Dacha asked Cass.

"If the alternative is returning to Sir Drex then I think we should try it," Cass said.

Dacha nodded, but his expression was unsure.

"I can go alone," Cass said.

"No," he said with a resigned smile. "We stick together." He paused for a minute. "There's just one problem. We don't have any skates."

"We can get you some easily enough," Riven said. "Food is short, skates are not."

"Thank you," Cass replied.

"But the first problem will be getting you out of Enzit," Riven said.

"I know, I'm sorry. I feel we have brought trouble to your door," Cass apologized.

Masha smiled and shrugged. "Don't worry, we are used to trouble. And I have an idea to get you out, although it's not particularly pleasant."

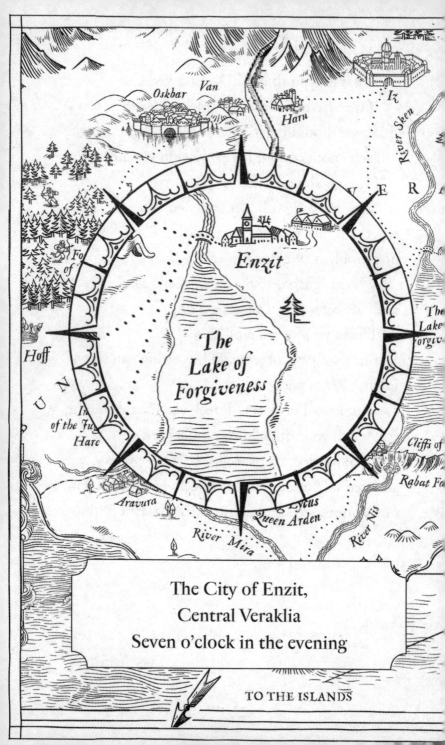

The City of Enzit,
Central Veraklia
Seven o'clock in the evening

TO THE ISLANDS

16

The Snowstorm

Not particularly pleasant was an understatement, Cass thought the following evening as she lay crammed in a coffin on the back of an undertaker's cart as it rattled through the streets of Enzit towards the city gates.

They had said goodbye to Idaliz at dawn that day, which had been hard for Cass. To be together and then parted again so quickly was very difficult and Cass had to stop herself crying. Dacha and she had then spent the day preparing to leave – assembling more provisions, going through their kit bags and adding certain necessities, all the while expecting Zirt and the soldiers to return.

They had eaten a meal in the late afternoon before saying goodbye to Riven. Then Masha had led them up to the top of the house and taken them over the slippery roofs, which Cass had found terrifying, to the undertaker's premises. He was a man of few words who had ushered them into empty coffins that were lying on the back of his cart, and after asking them to shut their eyes, he had placed silvers on their closed lids. He'd told them in a whisper that there were hidden air holes and the lids were not nailed down, so not to worry about suffocating but they must keep as still as possible. He'd taken their packs and hidden them in the front of the cart under some sacking.

They lay there with the noise of other coffins being loaded on beside them, which were presumably full of actual dead bodies, Cass thought, and she had to fight the overwhelming feeling of claustrophobia that threatened to engulf her. It took every bit of her willpower not to jump up and out of the coffin.

What saved her was remembering a trick that Idaliz had taught her, of taking yourself out of a situation by using the power of your imagination.

I am on a boat in the Far Isles, Cass told herself, *laughing with Rip as it speeds across the bright blue sea. I can feel the cool saltwater splashing on my skin, the warmth of the sun, the hot wooden planks of the deck beneath my feet. Look, there are fishes jumping out of the water, the volcanoes of Ra are ahead of me, how beautiful they are…*

Imagine it, imagine every detail of it, she told herself, as the cart drove slowly through the city, jolting over the cobbles. *The boat is coming into a harbour, the prettiest in the Longest World with white stone buildings covered in purple ischus flowers. There is an inn there that serves the most delicious crabfish fritters…* But Cass could not ignore the fact that the cart had come to a halt, probably at the city gates. There was the muffled sound of voices, which came nearer, and she felt the cart move under the weight of one or more people getting in the back. The Far Isles vanished entirely and Cass's stomach contracted with nerves as she listened.

"Here, I'll open this one for you," the undertaker said.

"You'll open all of them for me," a young voice replied. A soldier, Cass guessed, trying to control her panic.

"As you wish," the undertaker replied. Cass heard the sound of wood moving and the coffin lid being lifted next to her. From all the coughing and spluttering, Cass realized that there must be an overpowering smell. It reached Cass a moment later and she had to struggle not to gag.

The soldier swore and to Cass's immense relief, said, "Enough, old man. Take them away." The cart rumbled through the gates and out of Enzit on its way to the graveyard, which lay at the lake's edge, a mile or so out of the city.

Once they had reached the deserted graveyard, the undertaker helped them out of the coffins and handed them back their packs. People were so kind, Cass thought, as they thanked him. They risked so much for strangers and, as with Riven and Masha, Cass felt her thanks were inadequate.

"I think we should skate as far as we can tonight," Dacha said.

"Agreed," Cass replied. They made their way to the lake edge and put on the skates Riven had given them. The weather had turned fiercely cold again so there was no fear over the strength of the ice.

It was a clear night with a sliver of moon reflecting silver off the frozen lake. The lights of Enzit were clearly visible behind them but the lake's shore was shrouded in darkness. In the murky light Cass could see little of the landscape but every so often the shoreline would be broken by a grand staircase leading down to the ice, or ornate piers with carved wooden pillars jutting out, flanked by boathouses.

"What are these places?" she asked Dacha.

"They are the lake entrances of the grand summer houses of the rich merchants of Enzit. You'll be able to see them in the light tomorrow."

Dacha and she held hands for stability and speed. "We'll find some sticks to use as poles tomorrow," Dacha had said but Cass was glad of the comfort. There was something about the vast sleeping mansions that she found eerie and they made her feel twitchy and on edge, as if someone or something was about to come charging over the ice at them, like in a nightmare. It was only when the dawn came that she could see the buildings clearly, set back behind neglected ornamental gardens. They looked like abandoned relics from another world with their gaudy painted façades and shuttered windows.

They skated on, trying to put as many miles between them and Enzit as possible. *Will Nym and Zirt leave us alone now?* Cass wondered wearily. *Surely they have more important things to worry about with the invasion of Metrete?*

They passed a couple of tiny villages and saw a few people on the ice. Cass regarded them apprehensively but they didn't seem to stare back with any curiosity. They were instead preoccupied with the state of the ice along the lake. They greeted them always with the same words. "Is the ice strong?"

"The ice is strong," Dacha replied in an Enzit accent.

They eventually stopped around midday, when they both felt they really couldn't go any further. They ate some food and slept for a few hours in a disused boathouse. Cass woke up cold and stiff and alone and she felt a twinge of alarm. But then Dacha appeared, looking cheerful

"I've made us some sticks," he said proudly. He had sawn some oars in half. "It'll make us much quicker. Come on, let's get going."

While they had slept a blisteringly cold wind had picked up and when they looked behind them they saw an ominous bank of grey cloud massing at the head of valley. Dacha stared at it, frowning. "That looks like snow," he said with a sigh. And he was right, it was.

A fierce blizzard blew in, roaring along the lake like an animal and engulfing Cass and Dacha in a matter of minutes. Cass pulled her scarf up over her face to protect it from the stinging cold.

"We'll have to find shelter," Dacha called to her and they made their way off the ice and into the woods.

"There's a house," Cass shouted at Dacha, struggling to make herself heard over the wind. "I saw it ahead when we were skating."

"Let's go and look at it," Dacha cried.

The house and garden were separated from the woods by a high wall but as luck would have it they could see an iron gate set in the wall, not far from them. The gate was shut and very stiff but not locked, and with some pushing and shoving they got it open and made their way into the garden.

223

It was grandly laid out with walks lined with high hedges, providing some shelter from the wind.

"Shall we just stay here?" Cass asked, thinking that some of the hedges were so thick and ancient that they could crawl inside them and it would almost feel like being in a building.

"I think we should go and see if we can get into the house," Dacha said. "There are no lights on – I don't think anyone is there and it must be warmer than spending the night in a hedge!"

Cass laughed. "You're right, let's go and check."

They made their way on to the wide lawn in front of the house. The wind was screaming across it, hurling fine snow in their faces that burned like acid. They hurried up to the broad terrace that ran along the length of the mansion, where there was a line of French doors giving on to a large empty room. Cass and Dacha frantically tried the handles of each in turn. They were all locked.

"Nothing else for it," Cass said and shoved her elbow, well protected by her coat, into the pane of glass, knocking it out cleanly. She put her hand through the void and turned the handle. After a bit of shoving the door gave way and opened.

They almost fell inside.

The pair found themselves in a huge and magnificent room, with a high, coffered ceiling and elaborate wood-panelled walls. It felt so quiet and hushed that when Cass spoke it was in a whisper. "The ballroom, I presume, sire," she said to Dacha.

"Most certainly, Your Ladyship," he replied, also whispering. "Let's see if there is somewhere a little cosier. We'd better check none of the servants are around too."

After they had walked through a couple of empty rooms, Cass said in a normal voice, "Well, if they are, they aren't doing a very good job with the dusting."

Dacha burst out laughing, looking at the thick even layer that covered the floorboards like carpet, only disturbed by their footsteps. "I don't think anyone else has been here for several years."

"Shall we try and find the kitchen before the daylight goes entirely and see if they have left any candles or firewood?" Cass suggested.

There was the end of a stack of firewood by the dusty kitchen range and after digging around in the dressers they found some candles. Cass went into the larder and returned triumphantly clutching an old tin of tea and a couple of jars of jam, the only things not devoured by mice or rotted away.

"Now where shall we eat this feast?" Dacha asked, lighting the candles with his tinderbox.

"Let's go and explore," Cass said, and carrying as much firewood as she could she led the way back up to the hall. There was a grand marble staircase that wound up past a vast window to the floor above. Cass could see that the wind appeared to have died down but the snow was falling as furiously as ever.

They walked through a couple of large empty rooms that weren't particularly inviting. But then they came across a small room lined with books, which had a sofa in it. "Perfect," Dacha replied. "We can even use a few books to get the fire going."

This seemed almost sacrilegious, but then Cass found copies of some of the most boring books that she had had to read at Mrs Papworth's Academy. "Really we are doing the world a favour burning these," she said, handing them to Dacha.

The paper was beautifully dry and the fire was soon crackling merrily away. Dacha had brought a small copper pan and a couple of china cups up from the kitchen. He melted some snow from the windowsill in the pan and made some tea. Cass laid out all the food they had left on the floor in front of the fire. Four biscuits, a small amount of cheese and six strips of dried meat. Not much, she thought, looking at it with a pang of concern.

Dacha, seeing her expression, said cheerfully, "With the jam that is a feast fit for a Veraklian gold merchant. We will get some more food tomorrow. Now, let's eat and drink this tea." He handed her a cup. "It will make you feel better."

Cass took it from him and after a few sips and bites of food she did indeed feel more cheerful.

"This jam is delicious," Dacha said with his mouth full. He studied the label. "Rumberry jelly and this presumably is the Zama Estate. It says Drezen, so hopefully that means we are not too far from a village. I have silvers so we should be fine to buy some food tomorrow," he repeated in a reassuring voice.

Cass nodded, tiredness overtaking her. She scrambled on to the dusty sofa. "We mustn't sleep for too long," she muttered as she dropped her head down on to a cushion and shut her eyes.

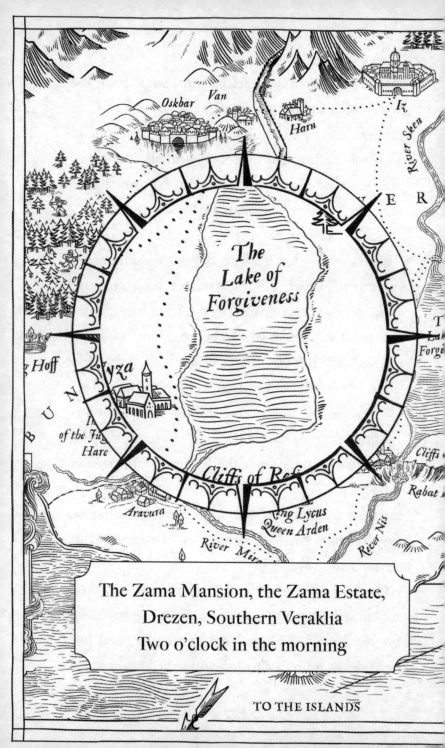

The Zama Mansion, the Zama Estate,
Drezen, Southern Veraklia
Two o'clock in the morning

TO THE ISLANDS

17

A Few Surprises

Cass never knew how long she did sleep for but when she woke up, the candles had gone out and the fire had burned down to a few glowing embers. The snow had cleared and the moon was shining brightly in through the windows. She looked out at the snowy garden, peacefully mysterious in the moonlight. Dacha was fast asleep, stretched out on some cushions on the floor in front of the fading fire.

Cass was just wondering whether to wake him when she heard a noise, a sort of scrabbling noise like an animal, and to Cass's amazement a small dog appeared in the doorway of the room. It stood for a moment staring at her and then came over and started to nudge at the back of her legs as if it wanted Cass to go with it. Expecting the dog's owner to appear at any moment, Cass dived into her bag and retrieved her knife. But no one came and there were no other noises, so she went over to Dacha and shook him awake.

"There's a dog," she hissed at him.

Dacha looked at her as if she were mad. "Where?" he asked.

"Right here," Cass replied. "And it wants me to go with it."

"There must be someone living here," Dacha said, jumping up and shouldering his bag. "We need to get out of here."

Cass grabbed her pack. She scooped up the jam, the tea and the last of the biscuits and stuffed them in it.

When they left the room, the dog assumed they had finally relented and decided to be led by it, and it bounded ahead of them down the stairs. They followed, heading back to the ballroom. But when they got to the bottom of the stairs and had a clear view into the room, they both froze. For the ballroom was full of people dancing, silently.

They were dressed in old-fashioned clothes and Cass, who had been subjected to hours of dance classes by Mrs Potts, instantly recognized they were dancing the four-way quadrille, a dance fashionable a hundred years previously. But despite the dancing, Cass could see that the dust on the floor remained unaltered. Her skin shivered with fear and all her instincts told her to run but she was rooted to the spot. Dacha, however, had no such issue and grabbing Cass's hand he pulled her towards the grand hall and the huge wooden front door.

They flung back the bolts and Dacha grasped the door handle to pull it open. Cass half expected it not to move, to be held by invisible forces, but it swung wide open.

Cass and Dacha charged out, sprinting over the snow, running as fast as they had ever run in their lives. They only stopped when they reached the lake. They scrambled to slide the blades into their skates so that they could get as far away from the house as possible.

"So being an obtuse clearly doesn't stop you from seeing ghosts," Dacha panted.

"Clearly not," Cass replied. Between gasps she added, "I've never believed in them before."

"I assume you do now," Dacha replied with a bark of mirthless laughter as they skated on into the night, not stopping properly until the dawn had broken and the world was once again flooded in daylight.

They ate their final bits of food but by midday they were ravenous. When they came to a village, Cass waited while Dacha went off to try and buy something to eat. He came back quickly with some bread and cheese and a few wizened apples.

"That's all I could buy, I'm afraid. It's the end of winter and no one has much in the way of food left," he explained.

They eked it out for the day and the following day repeated the exercise at another village. Here Dacha came back with even less. "It won't kill us," Dacha said. "We shall just be rather hungry."

Over the next three days they played a game, planning all the food they would gorge themselves with when they got back to Minaris, but then Cass decided it was making her even more famished. At least they were making good progress, she told herself, trying to be cheerful although the truth was that she was starving and exhausted. The weather turned milder and the snow from the blizzard melted. Small puddles of water were forming on the ice. Cass noticed that hardly anyone else was skating, and people started to shout warnings at them from the shore to watch out, the ice might break at any time.

When they stopped for the sixth night after they had left Enzit, they ate a tiny meal of stale biscuits and jam and made a meagre fire. Dacha said, "We have to get some proper food tomorrow, and the ice is melting fast. I have a suggestion. The next village along is Wyza, which is where the road loops down. It's much larger than the other villages and I think we could risk staying at an inn."

The thought of eating a hot meal, being able to wash and sleeping in a bed almost brought tears to Cass's eyes. "But won't we be too conspicuous?" she asked.

"I agree with Masha that Vegna and Nym's focus will be on sending as many troops as they can to Metrete. I doubt there will be more than a handful of soldiers there, if that. Anyway, let's wait and see – we should be there by the middle of the morning."

Wyza was set further back from the lake than the other villages, so they had to leave the ice and walk up a track to reach it.

"It looks more like a town than a village," Cass remarked as she caught sight of the buildings ahead.

"I agree," Dacha replied. "Do you think that means it might have a really good bakery with pies?"

Cass gasped. "And sugar buns? They might have sugar buns."

"Stop!" Dacha said. "My mouth is watering unbearably. It's like torture, and besides, we must stay focused. I may be wrong about the amount of soldiers."

"I agree. The thought of food, any food, is too distracting," said Cass.

They made their way through the streets, heading towards what they hoped was the main square, where they were most likely to find an inn and shops. They asked a boy for directions and he told them the square was just around the corner. *Thank goodness!* Cass thought as they turned abruptly into it and both stood stock-still, transfixed by the sight that greeted them. The square, which was huge for a town of that size, was jammed full of soldiers, standing around in groups, talking and smoking.

"Just act normally," Dacha hissed at Cass.

"But what in the Longest World are they doing here?" Cass muttered back.

"I don't know and I can't think straight until I've had something to eat. There's a baker's just here," Dacha murmured and they both dived into the shop.

The man looked at them wearily. "I only have some rye biscuits and they cost three silvers."

It was a ridiculous amount for dry biscuits but Dacha handed it over.

"I thought the army was headed to Metrete?" Dacha said to the baker, sounding as casual as he could while he handed the silvers over.

"Were they?" the baker replied disinterestedly. "All I know is that they have taken my bread and paid me a pittance for it. Anyway, what brings you two to Wyza?"

"Your famous biscuits," Dacha joked and they walked as calmly as they could out of the shop. They partially hid themselves in a deep doorway, and were both so starving that they shovelled a couple of biscuits into their mouths hardly pausing to chew them. They were stale and tasteless but neither of them cared in the slightest.

"That's better," Cass said in a low voice. "Now, we'd better find out what all these soldiers are doing here."

At that moment, there were shouted orders and the soldiers stamped out their cigarillos, immediately organized themselves into neat lines and stood to attention. There was a clattering of hooves and some way away from Cass and Dacha a mounted guard trotted into the square, flanking the unmistakable figures of Queen Vegna, Nym and behind her, Zirt. Cass and Dacha shrank back instinctively even though they knew they were too far away to be seen.

Vegna, dressed in furs and jewels and riding a white stallion, came forwards to address her troops. "Comrades, sons of Veraklia, my mighty army!" There were shouts and cries of approval. "Treasure this moment. You will be able to tell your children and grandchildren that it was you who made Veraklia great again! Our enemies – those land-grabbing, bloodthirsty Bundish, and those greedy Minarian fish – thought they could crush us, that we were defeated forever. But we have risen again, like a butterfly from its chrysalis! And what a beautiful sight you are!" There was more cheering. "So now, my friends, it begins. First we will take Minaris, something that I believe never will have occurred to that oh-so-clever Fish King," she mocked, to more laughter and cheering. "Then when Minaris and its riches are ours, we will take Metrete back."

As the soldiers cheered, Cass felt numb with shock at Vegna's words. They were headed for Minaris not Metrete. Nym had bluffed her and everyone else too. Idaliz, Sir Drex, Masha, Riven… They thought the army was headed to Metrete but it wasn't. They were going to invade Minaris and Lycus would have no idea. Cass's head swam with it all. What was more, she could see signs of enchantment on the soldiers' faces. Clearly Nym was leaving nothing to chance. Dacha, pale with shock, signalled for them to go, and while the soldiers were still cheering and applauding Vegna, they slipped out of the square.

"I don't believe it!" Dacha replied.

"We must get back to Minaris and warn Lycus as quickly as possible," Cass whispered frantically to Dacha once they were alone on the path back to the lake. "They have no idea what's coming."

"Do you think we should steal some horses?" Dacha said.

"Who from?" Cass asked. "The army will have taken every decent horse already. And we'd better not steal horses from them, it's too risky. How far is it to the border?"

"About seventy miles – if we walk or skate thirty miles a day we can make it in a couple of days."

"That's what we'll have to do then," Cass said. "Quicker if we can. We have to be faster than them."

Dacha nodded. "We'll be quicker on the ice, so I think we should skate for as long as we can. It's still very cold at night so the ice should be strong then."

However, luck was not with them. The temperature rose rapidly, melting the last of the snow and the lake ice, making skating impossible. So they had to march through the sodden woods, slipping and sliding in the mud. They hardly slept, pushing themselves on until they were, by Dacha's reckoning, only a mile outside Balzen and the border.

Freezing, exhausted and starving, they sat down on a wet log to share the last crumbs of the biscuits.

"I think we had better take the risk and go and see Masha's contact, the seamstress," Dacha announced.

"Do you think it's fair to involve her?" Cass asked.

Dacha sighed. "I don't know, but she is our only hope of getting back to Minaris."

Cass thought for a moment. In her heart she knew it was hopeless and that they would never get across the border but she felt she couldn't say this to Dacha. She couldn't admit defeat quite yet.

"You're right," she said, trying to sound as enthusiastic as she could. "We have to try."

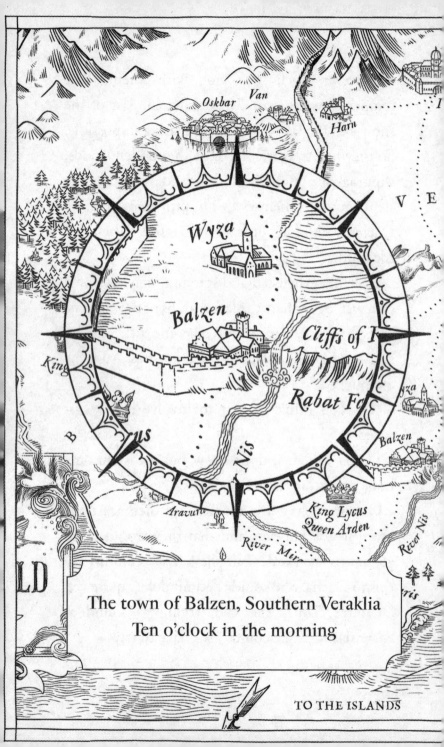

The town of Balzen, Southern Veraklia
Ten o'clock in the morning

18

Endings

The town of Balzen had the sad, neglected air that Cass and Dacha had become used to. Many of the buildings were boarded up and there were few people on the streets. But as Cass had predicted there were a large number of soldiers around. Cass and Dacha tried to look as inconspicuous as possible but they were still aware of being eyed curiously by the uniformed men. They crossed the main square and went down one of the alleys, following Masha's instructions, until they found the small shop, with the sign of a needle hanging above it.

The bell rang as they opened the door. The shop

was clean and bright inside, but there were only a few rolls of cheap material on the shelves.

"Hello?" Dacha called tentatively while Cass looked around. There was a clipping from a news sheet that had been pinned up, which caught Cass's attention. *Balzen heroine demonstrates new invention – "The Parachute" takes off!* And there were some pen-and-ink drawings of a woman dangling below what looked like a huge balloon. *Local seamstress Eva Traven demonstrates her amazing...*

"What in the Longest World is that?" Dacha said, looking over her shoulder.

He was interrupted by a voice saying, "Hello, can I help you?" They turned around to find a woman of about thirty-five eyeing them curiously. She was typically Veraklian-looking with red hair, fine freckled skin and large green eyes. "Can I help you?" she repeated.

"Are you Dorcas?" Cass asked.

The woman nodded warily and Dacha said, "We are friends of Masha."

Dorcas raised her eyebrows. "You had better come through to the back then," she said and

242

ushered them out of the shop.

She took them into a small parlour where there was a modest fire burning. There was a tailor's dummy, which was wearing a bright red silk dress of such lavishness that it almost took Cass's breath away. It looked so out of place in the simple room it was like coming face to face with a wild animal.

"It's for the queen," Dorcas explained. She produced a bottle and three small glasses.

"Apple brandy," she said with a smile as she poured the amber liquid. "I know it's early but you two look in need of it. And I always am these days." Cass took a sip and nearly spat it out it was so strong. But she could feel it warming her so she persisted.

"So who are you? Or is it safer that I don't know?" Dorcas asked.

"Perhaps better not to tell you anything," Cass said.

"Very well. Let me know how I can help you instead," Dorcas replied.

"We urgently need to get to Minaris," Dacha said. "Masha thought you might know someone who could take us? I have silvers."

Dorcas sighed. "I wish I did," she replied. "But I'm afraid it's not possible. Up to about three months ago there was some trading still, mostly black-market stuff, but a couple of official wagons went through with silks such as this." She gestured to the dummy. "Now it's totally impossible. The gates are shut and guarded twenty-four hours a day and the valley itself is patrolled constantly." Seeing the disappointment on their faces, she added, "Really, there is no way of getting through."

Cass took a deep breath. "What about going over Razat Falls?" she asked.

"In a barrel?" Dorcas asked, raising her eyebrows. "It's incredibly dangerous."

"I know," Cass replied. "But we're desperate."

She shook her head. "It's too early in the season. The pool at the bottom is probably still frozen and it won't have enough water in it. You would die for sure."

"Is there no other way?" Dacha asked her.

"You could go back across the lake and make your way over to Fricken and see if you could get over there. It would only take you ten days or so. Perhaps there might be fewer soldiers over that side of the lake. Or you could wait a few weeks here and then you can risk the barrel if you want."

"We don't have a few weeks," Dacha replied, with a sigh. "We have to get to Minaris before the army and they will be there in a couple of days."

Dorcas paused, looking at Cass and Dacha's disappointed faces. "I'm sorry to give you such bad news. Can I get either of you anything to eat? I don't have much but you are welcome to share it."

Cass was still thinking desperately. *There must be a way, there must...* "What about that thing? The thing in the newspaper cutting you had out there? Like a balloon..."

Dorcas looked at her quizzically. "You mean my sister's invention? The parachute?"

"Yes," Cass replied. "Couldn't I use that to jump off the cliffs and into Minaris?"

"Only if you were completely insane!" Dorcas laughed and then when she saw Cass was serious she said, "Really, that would be just as risky as a barrel."

"Cass, of course you cannot do such a thing," Dacha said. "Perhaps we should think about heading over to Fricken or even back up to Enzit…"

Cass ignored him, saying insistently to Dorcas, "Please could I speak to your sister?"

A look of grief passed across her face. "No," the seamstress replied. "She died, a year ago."

"I'm so sorry," Cass responded.

Dorcas sighed and thought for a moment. "I'll get the parachute down if you want and you can see for yourself how flimsy it is."

She disappeared off and Dacha said to Cass, "You cannot be serious? You could die!"

"I know, Dacha," she replied. "But unless I get across the border, Zirt will catch me and kill me so I'll wind up dead anyway. I would rather die trying to do something useful."

Dorcas came back into the room before Dacha could reply, carrying a canvas kit bag. She undid it, tipping out the contents on to the floor. It looked like an enormous puddle of pale-coloured silk. "This is it," Dorcas said, spreading the parachute out.

"How does it work?" Cass asked.

"A little like a balloon," Dorcas answered. "As

you jump the air inflates the parachute and slows you down."

"Where did your sister jump with it?"

"She jumped off some of the lower cliffs over by the border. I have to admit that her dream was to do what you are proposing. But then she became ill and so…" Dorcas petered out.

She was silent for a minute, thinking. "If you are serious, then I will take you up to the cliffs and I can show you the safest place that she had found to jump from. But first let us eat something."

Dorcas produced some stale bread and salted fish, which they ate accompanied by more apple brandy.

"So how did your sister come to invent such a thing?" Dacha asked Dorcas.

"Our father was a kite-maker," she replied. "He had the Veraklian obsession with the sky that Eva inherited. Even as a young child, she would spend hours throwing her dolls out of the highest trees in the orchard, trying to make them fly. And then when she was older she was jumping herself. She loved the feeling of having nothing beneath her, she said. It's as if you are out of time, in another dimension, even if it's just for a few seconds. Now, if you've both had enough to eat, let's go up to the cliffs."

Dorcas led them out of the back of her house and up a series of narrow paths, avoiding the roads. They carried the heavy kit bag containing the parachute between them and passed no one except an old lady, who stared at them curiously but wished them a good afternoon. On the outskirts of the town, the road, signposted for the border, snaked off to the right. But they took a path that turned left. It wound its way up through some woods, and then almost unexpectedly brought them out on a high plateau.

It felt like you were on the top of everything, Cass thought as the icy winds buffeted her. The Razat Falls were about half a mile to their left but the noise of the cascading water reached them, and down to the right the land abruptly fell away to the border.

"What an amazing place! I've never seen a view like it, even from the mountaintops in the north," Dacha was shouting to Dorcas over the wind.

"I know," Dorcas replied. "You can see why we

call it the End of the World."

Dacha gave a start and shouted at Cass, "Did you hear that, Cass, this place is known as the End of the World!"

"I'm not surprised," she replied, busy considering the jump. "I'm just going to have a look over the edge."

"But don't you remember what the fortune teller said in Oskbar?" Dacha shouted after her.

"Oh yes!" Cass replied and then laughed, saying, "Lucky I'm the one jumping then, not you!" She walked tentatively towards the edge of the cliffs, which were some distance away. With each step she felt more terrified but she forced herself onwards until she was only about a metre from the edge. The Minarian Plains were spread out beneath her like a picnic blanket, a thousand metres below. Cass felt a great tug of longing to be down there combined with an immense wave of shivery fear and nausea at the thought of jumping. Her legs felt strange and wobbly.

No, she thought, *I'm mad to think I can do this. I cannot. We will have to think of another plan.*

She turned back to join the others. They had

walked towards the woods but were facing Cass, deep in conversation about something.

Cass saw the horse and rider before they did. He galloped out of the woods, slicing the air with his sword as if he were in battle. Even from such a distance, Cass knew it was Zirt. He charged at Dacha and Dorcas.

The fortune teller's words to Dacha came back to Cass like a slap round her face. *At the world's end, you are in great danger...*

"No!" Cass bellowed as she pulled her sword out and hurtled over to them.

Dorcas and Dacha heard Zirt just in time. Dorcas screamed and sprinted back to the woods, dropping the kit bag. But Dacha flung himself out of the horse's path and then jumped to his feet, drawing his sword, ready to face Zirt.

At the world's end, you are in great danger.

And Cass ran like she had never run before in her life.

At the world's end, you are in great danger.

Afterwards, Cass would remember what happened next as both very fast and very slow. Zirt wheeled his horse around and reached Dacha in a few seconds. They fought, their blades slamming against each other. Cass was nearly there and was planning what she should do – a quick blow under Zirt's ribs, perhaps…

But then, somehow, Zirt knocked Dacha's sword clean out of his hands. Shocked, Dacha paused just for a heartbeat and in that hesitation, Zirt plunged his sword into Dacha's chest and his body crumpled to the ground. Cass knew from the way he fell that he had been killed instantly.

She felt as if the world had fallen away beneath her. "No, no, no!" she cried.

Zirt grinned at her.

That smile lit such a fury in Cass that she felt as if she would burst into flames. "Why did you do that?" she yelled at him. "It's me you want, not him!"

Zirt burst out laughing. "Oh, kitten, I'm sorry. Have I upset you?"

"I should have killed you in the Islands when I had the chance!" she screamed.

"But you didn't," Zirt replied, getting off his horse. "And now I'm going to kill you, Cassandra."

"I don't mind if you do," she replied truthfully.

But she was desperate for revenge too and so began to fight him with a cold, calculated rage that occupied every muscle, every sinew of her body. She cared nothing for her own safety; she only had one simple thought in her head, which was to kill Zirt. And so she took every risk, every gamble and it paid off. She caught him slightly off guard on a parry and swiped his sword away. She paused.

"Are you sure you have the courage to do it, kitten?" Zirt mocked.

Cass looked into his blue eyes, as she had all those months ago in the Islands. "Absolutely," she said and plunged her sword deep into his flesh.

Once she knew he too was dead, Cass could not help but fling herself on Dacha's body. *At the world's end, you are in great danger*, the fortune teller had warned Dacha. She had heard the words as well as him so why hadn't she reacted, why had she been so preoccupied and made a joke out of it? Why hadn't they left straight away? Or better still, why had she not agreed to stay with Sir Drex, as Dacha had wanted! It was all her fault, her own pig-headed fault.

"I'm so sorry," she whispered to the corpse. But it was no use, she couldn't bring Dacha back to life, she couldn't turn back time. *Oh, why didn't Zirt kill me instead?* She sobbed, so consumed by guilt and sadness that she felt her feelings would crush her down into the earth.

Cass didn't know how long she lay there with him but a voice said, "You must come with me before more soldiers arrive. You've killed a very important man." Cass looked up through a blur of tears to see Dorcas standing above her.

"I can't leave him," Cass cried, still clutching at Dacha's body.

"You must," Dorcas replied firmly. "He's dead, Cass, he's gone. As I said, others will soon come, so before they do help me get his body into the woods and then we can hide it and bury it later."

Together they carried his body as carefully as they could. Dorcas found a couple of fallen trees close together and they hid the body beneath them. "Now, will you come back to the village with me?" she asked.

To do what? Cass thought. To hide like an animal until she was inevitably found and killed by Nym or her soldiers. She couldn't run forever and she would only endanger kind people like Dorcas who helped her.

She shook her head. "I'm going to jump. I'll try and if it doesn't work so be it."

Dorcas wavered, wanting to object, but then seeing Cass's determination she thought better of it and gave a small nod in response. After Cass had taken one last look at Dacha, they walked back out into the open. The parachute bag was near Zirt's body where Dorcas had dropped it.

"Come, let us get it on you," Dorcas said. Cass stood still in silent shock at what had happened and what she was about to do. Dorcas took the harness out of the bag and tied it on her like a corset over her clothes. She then clipped the parachute on and gave Cass some instructions.

"I'll make sure the parachute stays on the ground until you reach the edge," she announced as she tipped the mound of silk from the bag and spread it out behind Cass. "You can steer a little by pulling down on either side, but mostly you just have to let the wind take you. Luckily it's coming from the right direction. Is that all right?"

Cass nodded and thanked Dorcas. "I will bring the parachute back to you. I will come back," she said.

"Come back in better times," she replied. "And don't worry, I'll see that your friend Dacha is given a proper burial."

The thought of Dacha being buried, Dacha who less than an hour before had been alive, filled her with such a wave of emotion that she felt it would sweep her off her feet.

"Ready?" Dorcas asked her.

If I die doing this, perhaps that is justice, Cass thought to herself. She nodded to Dorcas who held on to the parachute as Cass pounded along the ground and threw herself off the edge of the cliff with all her strength. The parachute fanned out behind her and the ground vanished beneath Cass's feet. Then there was nothing. Only the sound of rushing air.

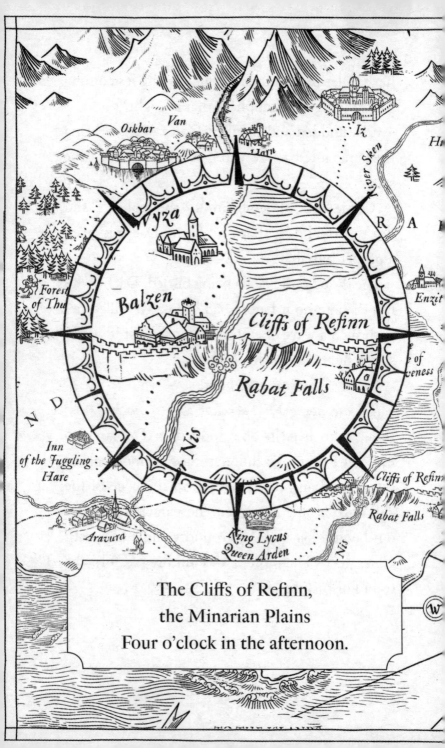

The Cliffs of Refinn,
the Minarian Plains
Four o'clock in the afternoon.

19

Minaris

The parachute carried Cass lightly away from the cliffs and floated gently down to the Minarian Plains. But for Cass there was nothing peaceful about those few minutes – all the raw anger and sadness spilled out of her and she couldn't stop screaming. The noise came from deep inside her and would not be stilled until she hit the ground with such a thud that it knocked it out of her. She lay on the cold wet ground for a few moments, staring at the sky where she'd just been. Her brain empty, she got to her feet, unhooked herself from the parachute and folded it up as neatly as she could. She hid it under a tree in a nearby copse, making a careful note of its whereabouts.

Then Cass began to walk. She walked through the evening and on into the cold, clear night, striding over fields and marshlands, only pausing briefly to drink water out of streams. Dawn arrived and she came across a track that she followed until a cart trundled past her, offering her a lift to the City of Minaris. She took it, sitting on the back of the cart until they reached the city around midday.

Without her citizen necklace, Cass had some trouble persuading the gatekeeper to let her in. But eventually he relented and let her through in the care of a palace guard, after she had insisted that she knew Captain Toskil and must see him at once. The guard looked bemused but showed her to the captain's room in the palace.

Captain Toskil was sitting behind his desk. He looked up when Cass was shown in and she could gauge from his expression of horrified concern how awful she must look.

"Cass!" he exclaimed, jumping to his feet and walking round to her. "I am so relieved to see you," he said. "Tea and Rimple's now! And some food," he barked at the guard who scuttled off.

"Come sit by the fire. Here, I'll help you," he said, leading her to a seat like a small child. When he'd settled her, he asked tentatively, as if some part of him already knew what she would say, "Where's Dacha?"

When Cass spoke she felt as if someone else was speaking. "Dacha's dead. He was killed yesterday by one of Vegna's commanders. A man named Zirt," the voice said, in a matter-of-fact way. She seemed to have rid herself of all emotion, she noticed, and felt only a sort of numbness. *What relief to no longer feel anything.*

Cass could see that Captain Toskil, however, felt a good deal, and it took him a few moments to master his emotions. "I see. How terrible. I must let his parents know. And the queen." He paused again. "Do you feel able to talk about what has happened?"

"Yes, but first I must tell you that the Veraklians are coming here."

"What do you mean?" Captain Toskil asked, looking alarmed.

"Vegna and her army. They are to invade Minaris, not Metrete."

"Are you sure?" Captain Toskil asked, looking even paler. "Our information from Princess Taryn is that Vegna is planning to invade Metrete. There has never been any mention of Vegna coming here."

"I'm positive," Cass said. "I've seen the army, heard Vegna say it. Her troops are mustering now at the border. They may have even started crossing. And she has a magician called Nym who is using magic, big magic. The whole army is enchanted."

"We must tell the king!" the captain said, taking her hands and pulling her to her feet. "This is a disaster," he said. "Almost all our army is up in Metrete with the Bundish."

I feel very strange, Cass thought as they walked along the marble corridors. Her head felt as if it were floating, disconnected from her body. She felt shivery and dizzy, and everything seemed too bright.

Lycus was in a council meeting but Captain Toskil interrupted it, saying he needed to speak to him immediately about a matter of the utmost urgency.

Lycus's pleasure at seeing Cass fell away when the captain told him of Vegna's plans. He too looked wide-eyed and pale with shock and asked

Cass if she was sure. When she replied she was, he instructed that riders were sent out to the border to see whether Vegna's troops had crossed yet.

"And Lin!" Cass said suddenly. "You must send for Lin!"

"The fortune teller?" Lycus queried.

"Yes. It is her sister Nym who's helping Vegna. Nym's very powerful, only Lin will be able to defeat her…" As Cass was saying this, she found herself violently shaking and she started to sweat.

"Are you all right?" Captain Toskil asked her, his voice sounding as if it was a long way away.

Cass was about to reply when she found that she was too dizzy to speak and the world disappeared in a storm of sparkling black.

She woke up to find herself lying in a grand four-poster bed, in a room lined with blue-green tapestries and a crackling fire burning in the grate. Tiger was sitting by the fire, sewing. It was such a peaceful scene that for a moment Cass felt at ease, but then all that had happened flooded into her brain.

"Hello," Tiger said, glancing up from her sewing. "How are you feeling?"

Cass sat up slowly in bed. "All right. Did I faint?"

Tiger nodded.

"How long have I slept for?" Cass asked, sitting up.

"A day," Tiger replied.

"A day!" Cass echoed, horrified.

Tiger smiled. "You were obviously tired, Cass. Now, you must eat something, otherwise you will faint again." She went over to a silver pot with a burner underneath it. "There's some porridge here for you," she said and spooned some into a bowl, adding cream and honey to it. She handed it to Cass who took the bowl and started to eat it. It was good but she could only manage a couple of mouthfuls.

"You have to regain your strength, Cass," Tiger said. "You're half the size that you were and there wasn't much of you to start with."

"I'm fine," Cass replied shortly. "I'm alive which is more than Dacha is."

Tiger's expression changed to one of sadness, and she swallowed before saying, "Cass, you must not blame yourself for his death."

"Why not?" Cass replied aggressively. "It was my fault that we were there."

"But you couldn't have known what would happen," Tiger replied evenly.

"I could have!" she almost shouted at Tiger. "We'd been warned by a fortune teller."

Tiger looked puzzled and Cass found she didn't have the strength to explain. The fight went out of her and she said, in a different tone, "I'm sorry, Tiger, I don't know why I'm yelling at you."

"You're angry, Cass, which is understandable. But I think you should try to rest a bit more."

Cass lay back and then became aware of a noise. It sounded like crowds of people some distance away. "What's that?" she asked Tiger.

"They are evacuating the city," she replied heavily. "Lycus's riders confirmed your reports of Vegna's invasion. The armies have been called back from Metrete but they will not be here for several days."

Cass was out of bed in a moment, crossing the room to look out of the window. A scene such as she had never witnessed before greeted her. The window looked out over the port, which was full, as was the sea beyond it, with hundreds of boats of every shape and size – from rowing boats to clippers, tugboats, barges, dinghies, galleons and skoots. The quays and surrounding streets were jam-packed with people, luggage carts, animals, birdcages…

"I should go and check that Mrs Potts and Tig are all right," Cass said.

"There's no point – you would never find them in that crowd," Tiger said. Then she added more kindly, "I am sure they are fine."

"Where are the boats going?" Cass asked.

"Mostly to the Near Isles. Loutrekia and Liversus will probably have to absorb the majority of people."

"Surely the queen is going? And you with her?" Cass asked.

Tiger smiled. "You missed Arden and Lycus having the most enormous row about it earlier. Arden won so we're staying. She's left you a note by the way." Tiger went over to the mantelpiece and picked up a folded piece of paper, handing it to Cass.

She opened it, and read,

Dearest Cass,

I was so devastated to hear about Dacha. How awful for you to witness his death. You must tell me everything when this terrible business with Vegna is over.

Arden

"Cass, I am sure a place can be found for you on one of the boats. It might be the best thing for you, to get away," Tiger said gently.

The daydream of standing on a boat as it cut through the blue-green tropical waters of the Far Isles filled her mind as it had when she lay in the coffin in Enzit. Rip was nearby and she could feel the warmth of the wooden deck beneath her bare feet, the sun on her face. How tempting it was...

"Cass? Do you wish to go?" Tiger asked, pulling her back to the present. Before she could reply, a bird flew past – an innocuous black bird – but it reminded Cass of Nym and then she thought of Dacha, crumpling in front of her. She burned with desire for revenge.

"No, I'll stay. When is Vegna expected?" she asked.

"Tonight," Tiger replied with a sigh. "Birds have been sent to the Bundish, Taryn and our troops in Metrete, but there is little hope that they will reach us in time. Anyway, Lycus insists that he will not hide in the palace like a coward, and will ride out to meet her in the morning."

Cass suddenly thought of Idaliz and asked Tiger if there had been any word from her.

Tiger shook her head in response before adding, "None at all, I'm afraid."

Please let her be safe, Cass prayed.

There was a knock on the door and Lin came into the room. "Cass!" she greeted her. "You're awake."

"I'll leave you," Tiger said and slipped out of the door.

Cass managed to give Lin a weak smile as she came over and hugged Cass tightly. There seemed to be so much to tell Lin that she didn't know where to start and instead she found herself saying jokily, "Well, I've found your sister Nym for you."

"So I hear," Lin replied. "I'm so sorry, Cass, about your friend."

Cass nodded quickly and changed the subject.

"Can you see what will happen? In the future."

Lin shook her head. "No. To be honest I don't want to look."

"Surely the Magical Enforcers will be able to defeat her?" Cass asked.

Lin sighed. "Almost all of them are in the Farthest Lands or up with the army in Metrete. Only Master Brackuz and a few apprentices remain here."

"And you," Cass said.

"And me," Lin replied. "But I doubt I have any sisterly influence over Nym. Also my magic is no match for hers."

Cass could see it was all desperate. "Do you know if Mrs Potts and Tig got off to the Islands all right?" she asked.

Lin smiled, relieved to be able to give some good news. "Yes, they were fine and, together with Tig's family, safely on a boat for Loutrekia."

"Good," Cass replied, suddenly feeling overcome with tiredness again.

Lin noticed. "Why don't you sleep? Lycus has asked that you and I accompany him to see Vegna in the morning so you should save your strength for that."

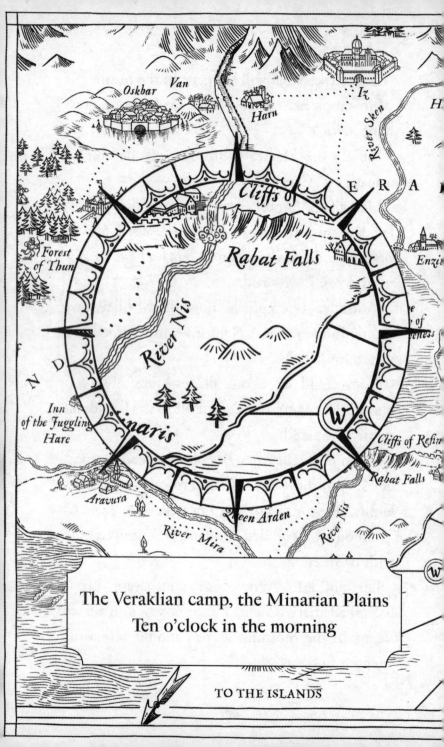

The Veraklian camp, the Minarian Plains
Ten o'clock in the morning

TO THE ISLANDS

The Magician's Battle

"Good morning, Lycus! Arden!" Vegna greeted them cheerfully as they rode up. It was a dull spring day, with a mottled grey sky and bitter east wind. The Veraklian queen was so enveloped in furs that only her small thin face was visible. Nym and the captains of her army flanked her and behind her was the sea of army tents that had grown up overnight like mushrooms on the plains outside Minaris.

She looks as if she has already won and Minaris is hers, Cass thought, taking in Vegna's breezy, confident air. Nym looked similar, but then Cass noticed the magician stiffen slightly when she saw her and Lin bringing up the rear of the Minarian party. *Good*, Cass thought.

"So, Vegna, congratulations!" Lycus began. "You fooled us into thinking that you were headed for Metrete."

Vegna smiled. "To tell you the truth, Lycus, I was. But then my friend Nym –" she gestured in Nym's direction – "changed my mind. For, once I have Minaris's riches, I will be able to take Metrete back easily."

"You seem to have it all planned," Lycus replied. "But what puzzles me a little is that you know we can withstand a siege for many months, let alone the matter of days that it will take the Minarian and Bundish armies to arrive. And they are a good match for your army, I believe."

He is pretending not to know about the magic, Cass thought, *to make her admit to it.*

Vegna smiled. "I may have a few tricks up my sleeve," she admitted.

"Oh, really?" Arden asked, feigning innocence. "Would you care to elaborate?"

Vegna glanced at Nym, who gave a small nod. Nothing happened for a moment or two but then the Minarian horses started to shiver and dance, unnerved by something.

Cass glanced down and nearly cried out in horror. For the ground was a mass of worms, beetles, spiders, millipedes, centipedes and other insects that Nym had summoned out of the earth.

"It will take more than a few conjuring tricks to bring down the Great City of Minaris," Arden said coldly, doing her best to still her horse.

"Those are no conjuring tricks," Nym replied. "As your advisors will tell you." She said the word advisors with a sneer.

Lycus and Arden glanced at Master Brackuz, who was looking furious. He replied tersely, "No, they are not conjuring tricks, Your Majesties. Commanding insects to do your will is most definitely classed as proper magic and as such is strictly forbidden. It goes against the rules set out in the Convention of Magic—"

He was interrupted by Nym scoffing. "Forbidden by the Convention of Magic – how terrifying!"

The Veraklians laughed.

"You can't do this, young lady!" he spluttered at Nym. "You cannot use powerful magic! I forbid it!"

Nym smirked at him. "Oh, do you really?" she mocked. "I am sorry to hear that. But I think the more relevant issue is who is going to stop me? We both know that the only Magical Enforcers with any sort of skill are not here." She smirked at Lin and Master Brackuz.

"Those who went to Metrete will be back soon," Lycus pointed out.

"They are no match for me," Nym replied nonchalantly. "And anyway, most of my work will be done by the time they arrive."

Master Brackuz coloured and blustered, "You won't get away with this!"

"Perhaps not in the long term," she replied. "But I definitely will in the short term."

"I think we're done, don't you, Lycus?" Vegna said. "Unless you wish to surrender now?"

"No, Vegna, I don't wish to do that," Lycus replied coldly.

"Well, I'll give you a few hours to think about it," she said.

Lycus made no reply. He wheeled his horse around and led the party back to Minaris.

"I need to speak to you," Lin said to Cass in an undertone when they returned to the palace and stabled their horses. Cass nodded.

"Come then, walk with me," Lin said, and she led Cass down towards the Quay of Disbelievers. The city was all but deserted now, with empty streets and shuttered shops. The quay itself, usually so busy, had a vacant look. As a watery sun tried to break through the clouds, they sat on a bench, overlooking the open sea.

"Nym fears you, Cass," Lin said.

"Perhaps." Cass shrugged. "She certainly went to a lot of trouble to capture me and the other obtuses. But she is also wary of you."

Lin paused before replying. "Her skill was always greater than mine, but I know I have a quality that she doesn't. It's hard to explain in words – a subtlety that she lacks that can give a greater accuracy in spells and their outcomes. However, there's no doubt about it – in a magical duel she is likely to defeat me. But that doesn't mean I do not wish to try. She has enchanted the army and I can even see traces of her magic in Vegna, so I feel there is some hope that if we can defeat Nym, we might at least give Vegna a moment's pause."

"Do you think that perhaps it will be like a house of cards – if you take Nym away, it will all fall?" Cass asked, feeling a glimmer of optimism for the first time in days.

"Possibly," Lin replied.

"But how in the Longest World can we get to her?" Cass replied. "She will be surrounded by guards."

"With a little magic," Lin said with a smile.

"Is this really going to work?" Cass asked. She and Lin were walking into the Veraklian camp as casually as if they were spending the afternoon strolling through a pleasure ground.

"Absolutely," Lin replied. "We're entirely invisible to everyone, as long as there are no other obtuses. But I think that highly unlikely – Nym would never allow one in her army. Remember not to bump into anyone, they can still feel you."

"Will Nym be aware of the magic?"

"Oh yes," Lin said. "The whole camp is covered with a web of magic. She will sense our coming like a spider who feels the tug of a trapped fly."

Lin was right. Nym was waiting for them, alone in her tent. It hadn't been difficult to find. It was large and nearly as lavish as the queen's enormous gold tent nearby, with a proper bed, rugs covering the rough floor matting, braziers and oil lamps suspended from the ropes inside. Nym was standing in the middle, smoking a cigarillo.

"Look who it is!" she said when they came in. "My beloved sister and the queen's flunkey. I presume this isn't a social call?"

"No, Nym. I have come to ask you to stop," Lin said.

"You have wasted your time then. Why in the Longest World would I stop now, just as I'm about to win?"

"Because you know where this ends. You saw what happened to our parents and the same thing will happen to you. The Magical Enforcers will eventually defeat you, then you will spend the rest of your life in prison."

"Not necessarily," Nym replied. "And even if I do, at least I'll have used my powers, not hidden them away like a dirty secret as you do, peddling tricks for pennies."

"I use my powers to help people," Lin replied. "Which is how they should be used."

Nym snorted. "You are living a half-life and you know it. Never really owning up to who you are. Our family were the greatest magicians in the Longest World and you have that skill and ignore it. Is that not a worse crime?"

"I don't think so," Lin replied. "You won't stop then?"

"No. If you want to stop me, you'll have to fight me."

"Very well," Lin replied.

Cass stood back with some apprehension. She had only seen magicians fight in a small way before and was uncertain what to expect. She watched, astonished, as Nym and Lin disappeared, only to be replaced seconds later by black amorphous shapes resembling thick smoke that could transform themselves into different forms. The shapes began as two bulky broad men, like the huge Suma wrestlers from the Farthest Lands. These shadow-wrestlers threw each other violently around the tent but neither appeared to gain the upper hand.

Then one of the shadows tired of that form, turning itself into a long thin tube that hurtled round the neck of the remaining wrestler. The wrestler immediately narrowed into the same form, twisting round the first one, as if it were strangling it. The tubes abruptly dropped down to the ground, changing again into tigers and fighting furiously.

Cass had never seen anything like it and watched with grim fascination as the shapes transformed once more into large orbs that careered into each other. This time though, she could see slowly but surely that one shape was getting the better of the other. *But who is it?* Cass wondered, praying it was Lin.

The shadows changed again, this time into huge snakes that reared up at each other like giant cobras. Then one pounced on the other, encircling and subsuming it. After a few seconds there was a shout of victory and the shadows were replaced with the figures of the two sisters – Lin was lying motionless on the floor with Nym standing over her.

Cass gasped and ran over to Lin.

"Leave her!" Nym shouted but Cass ignored her. Lin was pale as paper and her breathing was quick and shallow. *Alive but only just*, Cass thought.

"Leave her!" Nym repeated, grabbing Cass and pulling her to her feet. "Now, I've always wanted to see those famous circus skills of yours."

Nym undid a silk scarf from around her neck and it floated up into the air. Before Cass had time to react, the square of material hurtled itself at her, wrapping tightly around her face. Cass pulled it off but immediately it sprung back on, like a magnet to metal.

Before she could pull the scarf off again, ropes whipped around her, binding her feet and wrists.

"That's better," Nym said.

Just then there was a tentative voice from the entrance to the tent. "Your Excellency…" it began.

"Don't come in!" Nym ordered. "Just tell me what it is."

"The queen wishes to see you," the voice replied.

Nym looked annoyed. "Very well, tell her I'll be along in a moment." She turned to Cass. "Right, let's put you where you can't cause any trouble." With a slight movement of her finger, Nym flipped Cass upside down and hoisted her to the top of the tent so that she was suspended from the roof by a rope. Her sword slid out of its scabbard and clattered down to the floor.

"Oh, good, I wouldn't want you able to use that," she said. Nym looked over at Lin. She clicked her fingers and Lin was encased in a glass coffin.

"All safe and sound," Nym said with a smirk. "I won't be long," she added to Cass as she left the tent.

"No one is to enter under any circumstances," Cass heard her order the guards.

Being upside down for any length of time is extremely unpleasant as Cass quickly found out. The blood began beating violently in her head and with the scarf pinned to her face, she felt unbearably hot and claustrophobic. *My dagger*, Cass thought. *I have to get to my dagger.* It was tucked into the waistband of her trousers and Cass could just reach the very top of its handle if she really strained against the ropes.

"Come on," she said to herself as her fingers tried to grasp the top of the dagger and draw it ever so slowly and carefully out of its scabbard.

Don't rush! she warned herself, knowing that one hasty move would mean that it too would fall to the ground. Slowly she inched out the dagger until she had exposed enough to press against a section of rope. She began to gently saw through it.

Yes! she thought triumphantly a few minutes later when the rope came loose and she could free her hands. She pulled the scarf off her face and then, when it was determined to return, she managed to get it to stick to her stomach where it didn't bother her.

She allowed herself a small sigh of relief; she could breathe, she could see and she had her dagger. But she was still upside down, a couple of metres off the ground.

And that was where her circus training came in. Using all her strength Cass pulled herself up and grabbed the rope above her feet. With one hand holding on higher up, she then sawed through the rope, freeing her feet. Then with two hands back on the rope, she swung it so that she was over Nym's bed and let herself drop, landing as neatly as a cat on the mattress.

She ran over to Lin. How was she going to get her out of the coffin? And if she did manage it, how was she going to carry her past the guards? *Oh, what to do?* Cass wondered desperately. Perhaps she should go on her own now and fetch help…

Her thoughts were interrupted by a tut of irritation. Cass spun round to see Nym standing behind her.

"I see you are going to prove troublesome," she said, transforming herself into a huge mountain lion that roared and sprang at Cass.

Cass leaped to one side and dive-rolled over to her sword. She turned to face the lion, who was roaring furiously at her and pacing up and down, choosing its best means of attack.

Remember you are fighting Nym, Cass told herself, *who knows little of tactics*. So she launched herself at the lion, and with relative ease fenced it into a corner. It stood there, staring at her with its amber eyes.

I should kill her now, Cass thought. *It would mean that she wouldn't have a trial but it would be just. She has ordered the killing of many people, including Dacha, and her death would prevent a good deal more suffering.* Swallowing hard, Cass prepared to do the deed. She pulled back and was about to lunge when in a second the lion disappeared and there was Lion, the boy she had rescued from the pirate ship and loved like a little brother, standing before her.

"Please don't hurt me, Cass," he cried, cowering from her. Cass knew it was a trick but she still couldn't quite bring herself to harm him. She hesitated and the figure changed back into Nym.

"Oh, Cass, please don't hurt me," she mocked.

Enough, thought Cass furiously. She lunged at Nym with her sword but the magician disappeared again only to be replaced by the blue bird who shot up into the air. But Cass did just manage to clip her wing with the blade of her sword. The bird squawked and flew on to one of the guy ropes that spanned the tent. There was a moment's silence as both regarded each other. Then Cass heard a movement behind her and felt the point of a sword in her back.

"Cass, prepare to die."

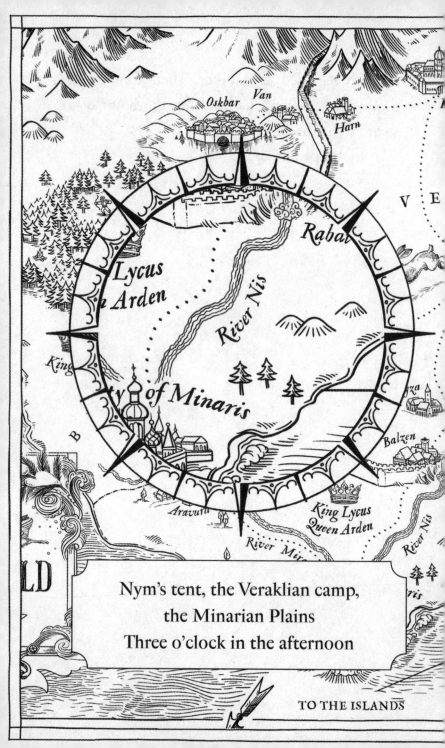

Nym's tent, the Veraklian camp,
the Minarian Plains
Three o'clock in the afternoon

21

Some Hope

Cass spun around to see Idaliz facing her. "What?!" Cass spluttered, looking at her familiar face. She could see that her eyes were clouded and her face was heavy with magic.

"You've bewitched her!" she shouted at the bird, who squawked back and then flew down to a chair, reappearing as Nym. The witch was pale and clutching her arm, which was bleeding furiously. *I must have hit an artery*, Cass thought, feeling a twinge of pleasure.

But despite the pain Nym must have been in, she managed to smirk victoriously. "I know and she's going to kill you for me. My guards found her trying to cross the border. Enough chat. Idaliz, please finish her off!"

"Prepare to die, Cass," Idaliz repeated like an automaton.

It was without doubt the hardest fight Cass had ever fought. Idaliz knew Cass's fighting style so well – her strengths, her weaknesses – and she could fully exploit them. Cass found it almost impossible to attack her with any conviction. Idaliz was her friend, and bewitched by Nym or not she remained that. Cass couldn't resist the feeling that she would rather die herself than hurt her. So she put up a poor fight and Idaliz soon had her in a bind that she couldn't escape from.

"Do you wish me to kill her?" Idaliz asked Nym in a strange dead voice.

Cass looked at Nym. She was sitting slumped in a chair, deathly pale, with her clothes soaked in blood. But she managed to say, "Yes, finish her off!"

Cass shut her eyes, preparing to die. She pictured Dacha and her parents. *Perhaps I will be reunited with them*, Cass thought, and it made her feel better as she braced herself for the pain of death.

But death didn't come. Nothing happened. Cass opened an eye tentatively and saw Idaliz gazing at her with a look of blank horror on her face. "Where am I? What am I doing, Cass?" she said in her own voice. She dropped her sword to her side. "I'm so sorry," she stuttered.

"It's not your fault," Cass said as she looked over at Nym. She was unconscious in the chair.

Then she heard a faint knocking. Lin had woken up and she gave Cass a weak smile. Cass and Idaliz rushed over, lifted off the heavy glass lid and helped her out.

"Are you all right?" Cass asked anxiously.

Lin was pale and shaken but nodded firmly, saying, "Fine." She looked over to Nym. "Her power has faltered."

"Will she die?" Cass asked.

Lin walked over to look at her, but then quite suddenly Nym disappeared. "Oh no!" Lin cried.

"What has happened?" Idaliz said, bewildered. "Where has she gone?"

"She has transformed herself into something

minuscule, too small for us to see, so that she can hide away while she recovers from her wound."

Cass could have wept with frustration. Seeing her face, Idaliz said, "Come, Cass, there was nothing else you could have done."

"I could have killed her before," she said, furious with herself.

Idaliz shrugged. "There's no point thinking such things, Cass. Instead we should focus on getting out of here."

"Are you strong enough to walk? And to disguise us?" Cass asked Lin. "Idaliz and I can probably fight our way out," she added.

Lin crossed over to a table where there were various bottles and poured herself a glass of Rimple's that she drank down. It brought some colour to her cheeks. "No, I should be fine," she said. "Let's try."

The camp was quiet and Lin's magic held. And the atmosphere in the camp had altered; a strong wind was blowing and the air felt lighter, as if a weight had been lifted from it. Cass dared to feel slightly optimistic.

"Will you go to the palace and tell Lycus?"

Lin asked when they were back in the city. She looked exhausted.

"Yes, of course, you go and rest," Cass and Idaliz reassured her and she left them to return to the Square of Seas.

"So what happened to you after Enzit? Can you remember?" Cass asked.

"I was captured at the border," Idaliz replied. "And would have been hung, if Nym had not realized who I was and intervened. I suppose I have to thank her for that. That's more or less the last thing I can recall. She must have kept me enchanted for the whole time. And what about you?"

Cass told her briefly about their journey down to the border, Dacha's death and then her parachute jump into Minaris.

"Oh, Cass, I'm sorry about Dacha," Idaliz said.

"Thank you," Cass replied, with that same feeling of numbness as before. "I ... I ... I don't seem to be able to cry about it. I mean, I could at first but now I just feel ... not nothing, but..." Cass petered out, unable to express herself.

"Sometimes that happens when you've had a

terrible shock," Idaliz said and she squeezed Cass's hand. "Don't be hard on yourself. Your mind will settle in time."

King Lycus was talking to Princess Taryn, who had arrived an hour before from Metrete with a handful of men. "Idaliz! I'm so pleased to see that you are alive and well," he greeted her.

"Only just," she replied. "And largely thanks to Cass. I'm sorry to interrupt, sire, but we wanted to tell you that the witch Nym has fled."

"Fled?" Lycus replied, looking amazed.

"Yes," Cass confirmed. "I fought and injured her, and she has retreated."

"But that's the most amazing news!" Taryn cried.

"It is indeed good news, but Vegna may still remain set on a battle," Lycus replied.

"But if she has no magic at her disposal, you can resist her until the Bundish army arrives," Taryn said. "They will be here in three or four days."

Lycus nodded and allowed himself a small smile. "Yes, possibly. Anyway, it is a matter for celebration. Let us all have a glass of winter wine."

They met at the same point on the plains as before, but this time Vegna's troops were arranged like toy soldiers behind her. She was on horseback flanked by her captains but Nym's absence was notable and Cass could see that Vegna, although she tried to disguise it, looked nervous. Her army looked ill shod and ill fed, and many of them were little more than children. There was also a slight air of rebellion coming off some of them now that they weren't enchanted.

Taryn had ridden out with Lycus, and Cass could see that her presence caused a strong ripple of emotion through the troops. And on Vegna, too; a wave of anger passed across the queen's pinched face. She greeted her with a curt nod.

"I hear you have lost your witch, Vegna," Lycus said. "What a blow for you."

Vegna gave a nonchalant shrug. "She was just one of my weapons. What is your decision, Lycus? Do you wish to surrender?"

"Aunt, can we not stop this?" Taryn said, nudging her horse forwards so she appeared to address not only the queen but also the crowds behind her. "I have spoken to King Lycus and to King Hoff. Everyone is agreed that Veraklia was punished much too harshly after the Magical Wars and they are happy to help us. They will send food supplies, and in the long term help us to mine more gold and give us fairer trading contracts. And Hoff is prepared to discuss a possible solution for Metrete."

"Oh, how very kind of them!" Vegna sneered. "I don't need their charity, Taryn. I have made Veraklia great again and I will make it even greater!"

"The Bundish army will be here in a few days," Taryn replied, again addressing not only Vegna but the troops behind her. "They will take back Minaris and kill much of the Veraklian army in the process. That is not what my father would have wanted," she continued. "And it is not what I want. I will be of age in a few weeks' time and the throne is rightfully mine."

"You're not in charge yet. You have shown yourself to be weak and disloyal, consorting with Veraklia's enemies." Vegna turned her gaze from

Taryn as if dismissing her, saying, "So, Lycus, you do not wish to surrender?"

"No," Lycus replied.

"Very well then," Vegna replied. "We will take Minaris."

"If that's what you want. The matter is settled," Lycus replied and he began to turn his horse round when something happened.

It started with a murmur and shifting of feet in the Veraklian army. Then a single voice shouted, "Taryn!" Another few joined in, then more, and in a matter of minutes the whole army was chanting, "Taryn! Taryn! Taryn!"

Taryn's face lit up. She smiled and raised her hand in salute to them. Vegna looked furious as her captains tried to keep order. But it was no good, she had lost them and she knew it.

Lycus, careful not to further damage her pride, offered his hand, and without a trace of victory said, "Come, Vegna, and let us discuss matters."

She paused for a moment, weighing up her options, then gave him a curt nod and together with Arden and Taryn they rode through the army to her tent.

Cass wasn't involved in the talks that followed. But she learned afterwards that it was agreed that Taryn would become queen, with Sir Drex helping her until she came of age, while Vegna relinquished all power. She would spend the rest of her days with the Mountain Sisters. Substantial aid was to be given by Lycus and King Hoff to the Veraklian people to get them back on their feet, and the most skilled geologists were to be sent to search for new seams of gold in the mountains. Trade agreements were drawn up while the Veraklians dismantled their camp, and a few days later they were gone, with Taryn leading them home. In Minaris, messenger birds were sent to the Islands telling the Minarians that they could return to their city.

"I must be getting to the Farthest Lands," Idaliz announced to Cass a few days later. She was holding a folded letter in her hands. "China, who heads up the Company at the moment, has written to me saying that the Magical Uprising is as strong as ever, so I'll join the rest of the group there."

They were sitting on the same bench in the Quay of Disbelievers that Cass had sat on with Lin previously, drinking glasses of flower beer. The harbour was still fairly empty but a few boats had begun to arrive back from the Islands. "I must start looking for a passage. Will you come with me?" she asked Cass.

I had almost forgotten about the Company, Cass thought. She had spent so long focusing on surviving and getting back to Minaris, and then on revenging Dacha, that all other thoughts of the wider world had been pushed from her head.

"Would you like to come to the Farthest Lands?" Idaliz repeated when she didn't answer. "Or why don't you come with me as far as the Far Islands and meet up with Rip there?"

Inevitably, Cass's dream of being with Rip came back to her but she pushed it away. She didn't feel like she deserved it any more now Dacha was dead.

"I don't know," Cass replied. "I think I should just stay here and help Mrs Potts."

"And be bored after about a week?" Idaliz said. Then she took Cass's hand. "You can't keep punishing yourself, Cass. It wasn't your fault. You have to let Dacha go."

"But I don't know how to," Cass replied simply.

"Perhaps you should go back and see his grave?" Idaliz suggested.

Cass nodded. "I've been thinking that."

"Shall I come with you?" Idaliz asked.

"No, thank you. I'll be fine on my own."

Later Cass went to the palace looking for Captain Toskil. She found him in his room.

"I need to visit Balzen," she said. "I have to return the parachute I used to its owner, and also…" Cass hesitated, finding it hard to speak of Dacha's death, as it still felt so raw for her. "Also…" she repeated, "I would like to visit Dacha's grave. So I wanted to ask if I could borrow a horse."

"Of course you can, Cass, but do you mind if I come with you?" the captain said. "I need to see where Dacha's grave is so I can tell his family when they return from the Islands."

Cass had wanted to go alone but the mention of Dacha's family made her think of them. Dacha had been her friend, but he was their son, his sister's brother. Their loss was much greater than hers. "Of course," she replied.

They arranged to ride out at dawn the following day but later Cass received a brief message from the captain saying that he'd meet her in Balzen the day after. Cass went to the stables, where to her delight she was reunited with Daisy, who was very pleased to be back with Cass, and even more so when she found they were going on a long expedition.

Spring had well and truly arrived on the Minarian Plains and the ground was covered in bright green grass, sprinkled with white melliflet flowers. The sun was in and out of clouds and although there was a brisk wind, it had lost its winter chill.

In the late afternoon, Cass reached the woods where she'd hidden the parachute. It took her a little time to find it and by the time she had dragged it out from under the log, shaken the dirt off and folded it neatly up, it was nearly dark. So she decided to make camp by the nearby river. It was a pretty spot, with a view of the Razat Falls behind. Cass made a fire and ate some of the food that she'd brought, then boiled some river water for tea. She drank it and lay back on a blanket to watch the stars come out.

"Over there – the mountain goat," she heard

Dacha's voice say in her head, pointing out the stars to her as he had that night when they were canoeing. "Do you see those two particularly bright stars? Those are the top of its horns and then can you trace down its nose?"

Cass yawned and shut her eyes, and something very strange happened. Afterwards, she would presume she had nodded off. It was the logical explanation but somehow it didn't feel like a dream.

Cass felt a hand on her arm, gently shaking her. She opened her eyes and found Dacha sitting next to her. He was dressed in his Queen's Guard uniform and looked as he had when she had first met him – healthy and well fed.

"What are you doing here?!" she spluttered, sitting up immediately.

"I wanted to see you." Dacha smiled at her.

"But you're…" She was about to say dead, but it sounded rude somehow.

"I am," he replied calmly. "But we both know that you can see ghosts. And besides, we never got a chance to say goodbye."

"I don't want to say goodbye! I want you to stay with me. Can't we go back and change things?"

Dacha laughed. "You know we can't. Come on, Cass, it's time."

"I'm not ready," she protested.

"You have to be, Cass," he said firmly.

"No," Cass insisted. She could feel tears beginning to pool in her eyes and then flood down her face. Dacha wiped them away with his hands.

"Tears are important but not too many and not for too long," he said. "I want you to remember that. Goodbye, Cass." He squeezed her hands with his, and then he began to fade before her eyes.

"No, don't go!" she cried desperately, clutching at the air where he had been. But Dacha had vanished.

Cass lay back on the blanket and cried and cried. Then when at last she was done, and her head was pounding and she was very thirsty, she walked down to the river to get a drink. The moon had risen and it was still and peaceful. And because it felt like the right thing to do, Cass said, "Goodbye," out loud, into the night. She took the silence that followed as a kind of answer.

Captain Toskil was waiting in Balzen with Tiger and Arden.

"If I come with Dacha's family it will inhibit them, so I thought I would say goodbye to him now," Arden explained simply and Cass could see she was right. Their day of mourning would become about the queen's presence and not about Dacha. But she was amused to see that Dorcas, when Arden introduced herself as just that, clearly had no idea who she was.

Dorcas showed them the grave in the burial ground. She had picked a good spot under an ancient tree that was full of memorial kites, bobbing in the breeze. Arden and Tiger had made Dacha a beautiful kite of fine red silk embroidered with traditional Veraklian symbols.

They took it in turns to fly it in the burial ground – it caught the wind perfectly, soaring and swooping up and down. And then Cass climbed up the tree with it, fastening it to a high branch, while the others prepared a picnic of ash cakes and a bottle of dark mourning wine, which they shared sitting by his grave.

They took it in turns to remember Dacha, and

as the day drew to a close they picked the creamy grief anemones that grew amongst the trees and covered the grave with them. After saying goodbye to Dorcas, they rode back to Minaris, each quiet with their own thoughts and memories.

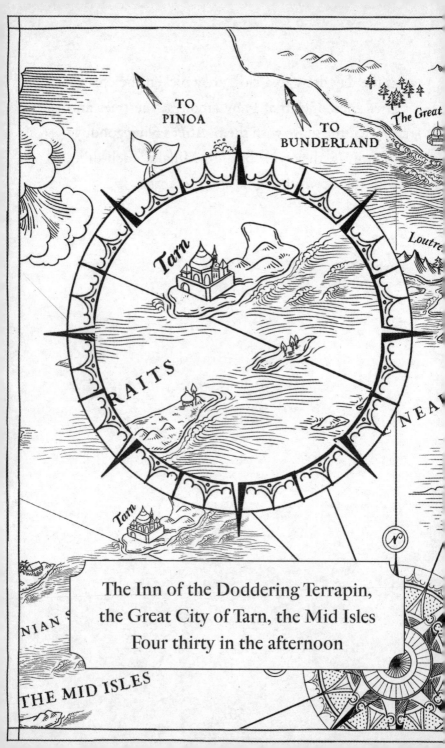

TO
PINOA

TO
BUNDERLAND

The Great

Tarn

Loutre

RAITS

NEAR

NIAN S

Tarn

The Inn of the Doddering Terrapin,
the Great City of Tarn, the Mid Isles
Four thirty in the afternoon

THE MID ISLES

22

Crabfish Fritters

"I am so enjoying my little holiday," Mrs Potts announced, taking a sip of bitter tea and Rimple's. She and Cass were sitting in the sun in the pretty garden of the inn in Tarn where Mrs Potts was staying.

After Dacha's funeral, Idaliz and Cass had boarded a schooner named the *Fish Bone* bound for the Far Isles. They had stopped en route in Liversus where Cass had been reunited with Lion, Tig and Mrs Potts. Lion and Tig had sailed back to Minaris shortly afterwards, but Mrs Potts had unexpectedly decided to stay in the Islands. She had discovered, rather late in life, a passion for travel and had sailed on to Tarn with Cass and Idaliz. "I think I shall make my way to Sedoor next," Mrs Potts continued. "And you're off to the Far Isles to see your young man?"

"Yes, although Rip's not my young man," Cass replied calmly. It was much too nice an afternoon to get annoyed with Mrs Potts.

"More fool you then. He's a lovely boy and has such beautiful manners. What's more Lycus is sure to make him Protector of the Islands in a few years time."

"Perhaps," Cass said, not wishing to get drawn into the conversation.

"What are your plans after your holiday?" Mrs Potts asked. "Will you return to the queen and Minaris?"

"I don't think so," Cass replied. "I think I may travel on to the Farthest Lands with my friend Idaliz," she said tentatively, expecting an objection from Mrs Potts to this course of action.

But to her surprise, the old lady merely nodded and said, "Well, dear, you must do as you wish. Now, let me pour you some more tea."

Cass left Mrs Potts an hour or so later. She walked through the streets of Tarn, enjoying the chaotic atmosphere and the sense of excitement that the city always had as the day faded into evening and the sky above her turned from blue to violet. It was full of clouds of swifty birds, circling around the city. It was so good to be back in the Islands, Cass decided. Although she still thought of Dacha much of the time, and had a sense of unfinished business with Nym, her brain was making way for other things and she could feel herself beginning to come to terms with what had happened.

Cass was heading to the Square of Obfuscation where she had arranged to meet Idaliz for supper. There was a food stall there that her friend claimed served the finest crabfish fritters in the Mid Isles.

But as she neared the square a young boy came bounding up to her. "Cassandra Malvino?" he asked.

Oh no, Cass thought, *not again*, her stomach

contracting, her eyes darting around looking for Nym.

"Cassandra Malvino?" the boy repeated.

Cass nodded, bracing herself for him to sing "Oh, I'm the Queen of Minaris…" But he didn't. He just handed her an envelope and ran off.

Cass opened it with some trepidation but inside was the Company's distinctive calling card – it was black with a figure of eight on it – and on the other side was written, *You are invited to a meeting of the Astrological Ladies at seven o'clock at Mele's house, 15 Street of Lions.*

The "astrological ladies" was the secret name that the members used for themselves and Mele was the original founder of the Company of Eight. Cass had visited her house in Tarn the year before with Rip.

That's strange, Cass thought. *I understood that, apart from Idaliz, the Company were all in the Far Isles.* But she shrugged off any misgivings.

It was only a little after six and Mele's house was just a short walk from the Square of Obfuscation so Cass wandered into the square with the intention of dawdling there for a while, enjoying the delightful jumble of jugglers, fortune tellers, acrobats, snake charmers, traders and food sellers.

She picked her way through, marvelling at the spectacle, and stopped to watch a couple of street acrobats. *My time on the Circus Boat seems like another lifetime*, Cass thought, without a twinge of regret. She walked on, waving away the fortune tellers, and then she was distracted by a snake charmer, playing his pipe, while the snake, a vicious black cobra from the Farthest Lands, rose up and up. While she was standing still, she was pounced on again by the street sellers.

"Look at the beautiful earrings I have…"

"Lady, will you look at the silks – the finest quality from the Farthest Lands…"

"No, thank you. No, thank you," Cass repeated politely.

"Here, smell my scents, the most exquisite," a man came up to her, boxes of glass bottles strapped to him, and waved a perfume under her nose. It smelt deliciously of orange blossom.

"You like that?" he said. "This one is even better," and he shoved another bottle under her nose. The sharp smell of etherine hit Cass like a blow, and before she could wrench her face away, she fainted.

She came round to find herself lying on her back on stone flags in the centre of a courtyard of a house. *Where am I?* She sat up warily, looking around her, looking for Nym. *She must have followed me from Minaris,* Cass supposed, with a feeling of awful, weary fear.

But the courtyard was empty and from the look of the buildings, the colour of the sky and the noise of the swifty birds, she was still in Tarn and only a short time had elapsed since she had been in the square.

A noise behind her made Cass start and she spun round, scrambling to her feet. A masked figure, a woman dressed in dark clothes, appeared, carrying two swords. Without a word, she threw one at Cass. *If Nym has hired an assassin to kill me why don't they just get on with it and not make me fight?* Cass thought with weary anger, as she caught the sword.

The fight began. *Whoever she is, she fights*

beautifully, Cass appreciated, as the woman engaged her in a parry and nearly knocked her sword out of her hand. Cass rallied and they began again, but this time Cass had a sense of the woman taking a step back, almost observing her. *Is she playing with me, like a cat does with a mouse?* Cass was distracted, leaving herself undefended in a move. The woman flipped her sword out of her hand and it clattered to the floor. Cass dived for it, but the woman's sword was at her neck before she reached it.

"That's enough, Cass," she said calmly and then withdrew her sword saying, "You can get up now." Bewildered Cass got to her feet as the woman called out, "Your protégé fights well. You can come out now."

To Cass's surprise, a doorway opened and Idaliz appeared. "But what…" she stammered.

The woman took off her mask, put away her sword, removed her gloves and offered Cass her hand. "I am China, one of the few members of the Company that you haven't met."

"How do you do," Cass replied stiffly, shaking her hand. She was still mystified and slightly annoyed. "I thought you were all in the Farthest Lands?" she queried.

"I was, but I wanted to come and meet you," she replied.

"But why did you kidnap me? I was coming here anyway," Cass said, unable to hide her irritation.

"I am sorry, I wanted to take you entirely by surprise to see how you fought. So please accept my apologies and I hope it will not mar our evening, for I have a problem that I am hoping you might be able to help me with. But shall we discuss it over some supper? I'm starving."

"Of course," Cass replied and followed Idaliz and China through a doorway into an adjoining courtyard. It had a mulberry tree at its centre and Cass instantly recognized it as the courtyard in front of Mele's house. A table had been set up with plates of crabfish fritters and a jug of summer wine. China poured them all a glass and they sat down together.

Once they were settled, China began, "So, Cass, my problem is that Ada, another member of the Company who I think you met some time ago, has fallen in love with a peach farmer in Villuvia and wishes to leave us. I am of course delighted for Ada, but it means there is a space in the Company that needs to be filled. Various names have been put forward but it's yours that keeps cropping up." China took a sip of wine. "I wanted to find out if joining the Company was something that you might be interested in. As I'm sure you know it's dangerous, secretive work and your life is not entirely your own. If you do decide to join you have to swear allegiance to us and our principles, and you'll be sent where the Company decides the need is. So, what do you think? You don't have to decide now, but is it something that you might be interested in?"

Cass was so excited she could hardly find the words to reply, but somehow she managed to stutter, "Yes! I would be honoured to join."

"You're sure? Don't you want to think about it?" China asked.

"No, I don't need to think about it at all – I am absolutely positive that I would like to join," Cass replied.

"Good!" China exclaimed as Idaliz cheered loudly. "There is the small matter of your oath and then a tattoo at a later date, but I think we should eat these crabfish fritters first. Idaliz tells me they are the finest in the Mid Isles."

"They definitely are," Idaliz said. "And I think we should toast Cass."

"To Cass and her long and glorious future with the Company!" China cried and they clinked glasses.

Above them the violet sky darkened and the clouds of swifty birds circled above the rooftops around Mele's house, before heading back to the Square of Obfuscation. A man, standing in the attic window of a nearby house, inspected them with his spyglass. Birds were his passion and every evening he watched them from his window. But as he gazed at their antics, he nearly dropped his spyglass in surprise. For there, among the grey birds, was a single bright blue intruder. He recognized it immediately. A woodland warbler. *How amazing to see one so far south*, he thought and then smiled, remembering their reputation. "What a lucky omen it must be!" he murmured to himself.

Acknowledgements

A massive thank you, as always, to my brilliant agent Catherine Pellegrino, for her invaluable advice and support. Huge thanks to the whole team at Stripes, particularly my editors Ruth Bennett and Mattie Whitehead, whose creative and patient editing has not only transformed the book but also made the whole process such a pleasure.

Many thanks to Pip Johnson for creating such a fine looking book, to Maria Surducan for the beautiful cover and to Charlie Morris, for masterfully launching it into the world. Ella Whiddett, Elle Waddington and the Rights team – thank you for all your hard work. And finally, I want to include a shout out to all the book bloggers, teachers, booksellers and librarians who have been so supportive of my books – your help is greatly appreciated.

Harriet Whitehorn grew up in
London where she still lives with
her family. She is the author of the
Violet series, which was nominated for
several awards including the Waterstones
Children's Book Prize, and the Freddie's
Amazing Bakery series.